B.O.W.

BITCHES OVER

Wives

MELISSA COBB

Changing The Heart Publishing

PUBLISHER'S NOTE

Editor: Linda Corley

Printed in the United States of America

STATEMENT

"It didn't use to be this way, but along the way it became that way. In fact, out of misery a bitch can be born to show you just because you are good, you don't always win."

MORAL STATEMENT

"What power does another woman think she has on your husband (man)?"

B.O.W.

(Bitches Over Wives)

A

Novel

MELISSA COBB

CHAPTER 1

THE CONVERSATION AND REASON THAT STARTED IT ALL

"You skinny-looking high-classed bitch!"

"Whoa, I thought you were saved on my line saying the B-word."

"I am saved. I am tired of you toiling with my life and playing with me as if my husband is a game."

"Why play with your husband when I can have him?"

"You can't have anything but a bullet in your heart."

"And it's made of stone."

"You insincere."

When she said, "You insincere" I cut her off by saying, "Listen, I'm not letting anything or anyone, wife or not come between me and that money. But today I am feeling generous. I know it is your daughter's sixth birthday; therefore, I will allow him time to attend the party and, after the party is over, that dick comes back to me."

With an attitude I expected her to have she stated "You will not tell me about my marriage, my family time, and especially about my husband. Hear me this day I am tired

1

of you and the things you try to pull. You are not his wife but a wannabe. And if I wasn't trying to be saved, I'll."

I cut her off and spoke tauntingly, "You won't do anything. Look, I was feeling generous, and feeling is sensations that can leave at any time. You keep running your mouth your daughter will be sad because her father won't be there to watch her blow out the candles on that princess cake you bought."

She did a laugh that sounded like she was angry but trying to hold back. She used assertiveness as she stated, "You, on the other end of this phone, trying to wreck my daughter's day; then you have the nerve to tell me what I need to do about my husband. The man God gave me. I am the wife, not the side piece."

"He spends more time with this piece than he does with your piece. Not only that, I am woman enough to fuck my man, and you will be woman enough to let me fuck your husband, my man Barb; if that is what I so chose to do."

Her voice peaked as she said, "It's Sister Barbara to you and I don't think that will even go down like that. If anything, you need to get with Jesus and make him your man. So you can stop playing with other women's husbands."

Not caring what her name is, I spoke casually "Sister, if you were doing your job, I wouldn't have to get paid to do it for you."

She tried to out-talk me, but I put a little base by saying, "Control your damn tone. I'm speaking."

She tried to loud talk again, and I started again but a little louder over her voice to say, "I said to control your damn tone, I'm speaking. If you shut the hell up, I'll let you speak."

His wife became quiet, and I said, "Now you may speak."

She sounded as if she was talking through her teeth, "You won't ever be a wife. Whenever you have your husband, you will always want someone else's, but you can't have what is promised to me. What God put together, let no man put asunder."

Shutting her down quickly I spoke casually, "I'm not trying to put asunder any marriage, but you need to let him know that he is promised to you and not to me. As much as he is at my place, one would believe he belongs to me and not you. But it's funny you should say that I won't ever have my husband. Because I am a wife, but why be the wife when I can be the bitch that gets more than the wife?"

I listened as Tony's wife Barbara tried quoting a scripture, "The Word tells you, thou shalt not commit adultery and that goes for you and my husband. If you think you are going to get by with this, you are wrong. You will pay for being involved with a married man and many problems will be added onto you, if you don't die and go to Hell first."

3

To mock her, I spoke as I rolled my eyes, "Ain't nobody talking about going to no Hell or dying for being involved with a man his wife can't please."

"Vengeance is the Lord's, and he will repay but if I wasn't trying to live saved, I'll put a bat in your face and these eights on your back; and I put that in Jesus' name."

Being cocky was a characteristic I learned and for that, I responded, "Your problem is not with me, it's not even with Jesus. It's with him; my money man the one you call a husband. But when you want to add to me, you better learn how to subtract yourself from me because I promise you, this ain't what the fuck you want."

Not giving her time to retaliate, I hung up as Josiah and I settled on the United Airlines first class seats. The flight attendant offered a soda, and I got Josiah a blanket. He nested into his seat as I pat him to sleep. Soon as we took off, I stared at my son and thought how I had never been one to mess around or be strong enough to front a woman about a man; a husband at that.

However, women need to learn how to use the power they have before another one uses it for them. I thought about myself, and the power I didn't know I needed until the day I lost it. Closing my eyes on the plane, I laid back and recalled *how it was the day I was riding in my car to our church God's Spoken Word in Louisville. I had the feeling that something was off as I waited for my fiancé to come home. It was late and he was due from his bachelor party. The moment I saw his face with tears in his*

4

eyes, I immediately felt hopeless.

Ahmad gave me a faint smile as he said he wanted to sing to me. I know he can sing like bird and for him to want to sing to me was his way of expressing himself. Those lyrical words coming from his lips moved me to tears; even though, his voice was sketchy. Shortly after, he finished singing he leaned on my shoulder and cried like a baby. I placed my hand on his head to question him what was wrong.

He only replied that his life has changed, and he can't do anything about it. I did not understand what he was telling me because the last time he cried this sorrow stuff was when his mom passed away, and that broke him down. He became very distant from me and would not allow me to comfort him in any form. With Josiah being a small baby, I was already in a state of being overwhelmed, and I too needed someone but had to be strong because Ahmad needed me more than I needed me.

Placing what I was going through to the side, I tried being there for him. Although, nothing I did work and nothing I tried helped. Ahmad began drinking heavily when he got off from work, on the weekends, from sunup to sundown, and hanging with worldly guys from the job. He stopped talking to me and jumping from my slightest touch. He even started smoking marijuana and cursing as he became complacent in the things of God.

No matter how I prayed about his behavior, he seemed to get worse. I felt like the more I talked to the

5

Lord, the stronger the evil spirit in him would get. Nothing worked as I fasted and cry out for my love. I even stood in the gap for him to come back to the Lord, but nothing changed. I got annoyed with reasoning with him about how worldly he was becoming; therefore, I kept my peace.

As much as I could I kept reminding him that the Cross of Jesus is the answer to whatever he was going through he would ignore me. I kept reminding him that Jesus loves him, when he feels like no one does but that did not move him. My last resort was to have the devil cast out of him, but he was quick to say a Holy Ghost-filled Christian can't be possessed by the devil.

The enemy cany indeed can use the child of God but he can't live in the body of a true Holy Ghost-filled believer. Because your body is the temple of God and if his Spirit lives in you, the devil can't live there either. So, getting him to admit he had a problem was not going to happen. I had to think of another alternative.

Many things rushed through my mind about why he was taking a turn towards the world. My focus became anxiety because we were getting married. He convinced me that marrying me and being a more involved father to our son was the upmost important thing in his life. He concluded that working longer hours at Taylor's and keeping things going was stressing him.

Inwardly I was unsatisfied with him because of the emotional neglect, he gave me. I even asked if getting bigger was an offset, but he guaranteed me that I was still *his one love. If he hadn't changed to a worldly man, I would have been okay. Because of this change, the idea of him cheating crossed my mind.*

That thought had me worried as I listened to my inner female judgment. As luck played a chance one day, I broke his code and began tracking things he did on Facebook, recent calls, photos, and phone records, in case he erased numbers out his phone. I even went over to the search part of his phone and typed in words, in hope to see any messages from anyone of long ago.

Soon those ended in a blank. Now I am looking at me, for nothing was found on him. I had assumed I was the one being different because everything happened so fast, with our son being born and his mother's death. It was easy to be distracted and see things differently, but I needed to make sure that I hadn't blamed anything that looked like a problem.

But all the things he told me lined up and no holes were found; therefore, I dismissed the fact that another woman could be involved. Before I realized it, the old us were back but better. We started making love more and sending each other love texts. Our quality time was up.

When he wasn't at work, he was at home, and when he wasn't at home we were at some type of church function or his dad's house. During this time, he came out and told me that this acting out was his way of coping with being a family man and his mother's death. I became okay with it. I was willing to do and attempt anything to keep him smiling.

Nothing was the limit when it came to this man and my love for him and our son. Since that day, Ahmad was happier and living healthier when it came to the things of God. Josiah, our son, was a little over two when we finally had the engagement dinner at the Citizens Bank off Main Street. I must admit I was more nervous than he was but excited about the wedding. I had smiled as my thoughts were of the man I had loved my whole life.

Ahmad and I were each other's first everything and every memory in my life in some form has him and J Lamb in it. It is here, I thought about Jamal my best friend whom I call J Lamb. This crazy guy introduced me to his brother. We were in the ninth grade and Ahmad was in the tenth at Ackerman High School, and since that day we have been inseparable.

Many a day, we had walked up and down the streets in Choctaw County. There wasn't anything about me J Lamb didn't know, and there wasn't anything about him that I didn't know. Even when I had my doubts about Ahmad, I talked to J Lamb. He would tell me that if his brother is fucking any bitch, I better be the bitch he doing and from the way he talks, you knew he did not walk in the ways of the Lord.

But that never discouraged me from being his friend nor once stopped me from telling him from time to time he needed to come to church. Just mentioning the word church made my eyes water. I got a napkin from the flight attendant and wiped my eyes. Josiah was asleep. *I begin to*

8

think about my wedding day. I remembered how J Lamb appeared happier than I did.

I had arrived at church, and my sister-in-law Jessica hugged me as J Lamb spoke loudly and in his usual slang, "If it isn't the most sought-after bitch in all the land. Today's your day, Tiger Ho."

I began to laugh. He has always been the only one to ever use my name in such a manner. J Lamb gave me that nickname because he could not say my first name, which is Tygeria, and the Ho came from my last name first initials Homely. It was always funny to me. Seeing my other best friend in the entire world, as he spoke, "That is the smile I love to see, and I am so glad my brother will be seeing that smile. You know you always talked about God and stuff, now you can stop shacking."

"Oh, you do listen?"

"More than you think I do. Between you and daddy I can't help it. I hear it at his house. I hear it at your house. Sounds like to me I need my own house, don't I?"

"You can't make it in your own house."

"I know that, and you know that that's why I stay with y'all."

He put picked up my bags as Jessica, took Josiah off with her to dress him. J Lamb and I went to the church dressing room. I opened up the door, they're shining like a new coin on the rack was my dress. The off-the-shoulder

9

dress with lace and diamonds screamed, expensive. Just seeing how that one piece alone can make a girl's dream come true brought tears to my eyes.

It is the most extravagant piece of clothing I have ever bought, and today it will be worn for the man I love. In his country voice, J Lamb halted my admiration by saying, "Girl that thang pretty."

"I know. It took all the extra doe I had in my savings for this dress and just for today."

In his cheap tone as always, he spoke as he walked off, "Ain't no way I would spend countless dollars on a one-day event. I would have gone cheaper and rented the dress."

"Rent me."

"No, no, you in church," J Lamb said to remind me about my choice of words.

I gave him a playful shrug he set my bags on the floor, and I laughed more. I never would forget his words as he spoke, "Tiger, you have been my best friend, and I am so glad you are going to be in my family forever. I mean even if my brother doesn't act right, you still my favorite."

I shook my head and finger to politely remind him with a tease, "No, no, don't say that. We're in the church remember, and it is my wedding."

He said, "Girl, this wedding needs to hurry the heck

up. I don't know how much longer I can contain my tongue."

"You are so right."

"Where is the honeymoon going to be, so I can come crashing it?"

I laughed as I stated, "I told him to go to the Casino in Philadelphia. It's close by, and we have work on Monday."

"Y'all don't gamble."

"You don't have to gamble to have a wonderful time."

"If you ask me, y'all wasted a lot of money on this one-time event, that's if you ask me. Hell, I mean, heck, y'all been together forever. The only difference is you add his last name to it. When all y'all had to do was go to the Justice of the Peace and ball out on a reception."

"Ain't nobody going to a courthouse to get married by some man they don't know."

"True. Daddy would have died and burst hell wide open before someone you don't know married y'all. Shoot, wait 'til I get married."

"I would love to see the day you get married."

"Tiger Ho, you and me both."

We laughed more as he began to do my hair and make-

up. The more I sat there, the more J Lamb and I talked and talked and talked. It seemed like forever on that day he and I chatted like this. We understood that our different lifestyles have separated us, but we don't see it as a downfall. We see it as doing our own thing, making our choice in decisions.

Soon as he finished with me, he went to get dressed. My brother came in and brought my son to me. I wanted to cry because Josiah was so handsome with his little tux on. He is the spitting image of his dad Ahmad but a lot younger. I gave my son Josiah a peck and he said, "Mommy pretty."

Josh's wife Jessica came in and took my little man back with her. I assumed that my brother wanted to have a few words with me before he gives me away. Soon as the door was closed, Josh said with tears and a smile, "Sis, I didn't come in here to give you a speech but here I am. I am thinking of all the things a man would say to his daughter. You have been like my daughter, and I have always watched over you as such. I am so happy for you. You have grown into such a lovely young lady, and you exemplify yourself in such a way that I am honored to have been a part of your life. At the same time, it pains me to let you go, but I know I am letting you go into the hands of a man that has proved himself to be worthy of your love and my trust. You will make a great wife to him, but if he steps out of line, I will be there, and he's not going to want me there. You and Josiah are my only living family. All the loved ones we know are gone on and today, Ahmad will be *added to the list of family. He will be the brother I never had."*

Just seeing my brother like this being the big brother he is made tears form. He has always watched out for me and even been over-protective from time to time, but that is what family will do for each other. In part, you can say he raised me on up until I turned twenty-one years ago because our parents passed away due to a car accident through no fault of their own. I was twelve, and my brother was twenty-three.

Josh instilled values of family and tradition that our parents taught us. He put me through school and has always been there for me. My brother has been the type of man, I wanted to marry, and today I am marrying a version of him. I didn't want tears to fall but they were trying to come as I said, "I know it seems like a dream come true to me. I just wish our parents were here to see what a great job you have done to be a brother and provider for me."

"Don't cry, Ty you'll ruin your make-up then J Lamb would have to fix you up in a hurry."

Grinning I said, "Josh, I can't help it this is one of the happiest days of my life and our parents aren't here to share it with us."

"Think of them as here in the both of us and in spirit. They have always lived the way of the Lord so, I do not doubt that they aren't there looking down on this special moment."

I chuckled a light laugh then spoke, "Just wish they were here in body form."

"Ty you are a wonderful mother to your son, and you will be a greater wife to your husband, as long as you don't lose focus on God and go to him in everything you will be fine."

A knock was heard at the door, and I spoke, "Who is it?"

"It's the only good-looking man here at this occasion."

Wiping away more tears, I spoke with a smile, "Come in J Lamb."

"Hate to break up the chit-chat, but it's time for you to be in my family."

Josh looked at me and asked, "You ready?"

"Nervous, but yes."

With cheer, he responded, "Come on, let's get you married."

We walked out of the dressing area and stood in the entrance hall of the sanctuary closed doors. J Lamb looked at us and whispered, "I love this part."

When J Lamb pushed open the doors, he revealed us at the beginning of the aisle. Soon as we were seen, the music began to play. We have been over this part a million times

14

and each time I said I wasn't going to cry. But that day it was real, and I was crying as I heard "All My Life" by K. C. and Jojo. I took the napkin from my hand, patted my eyes so my mascara would not ruin my make-up. I had tried to hold in my emotions, but that was the moment I had been waiting for, and it was finally here.

The slower my brother walked me down the red carpet with my long off-the-shoulder gown, I was thankful that my veil covered my face. I had been through so much with this man there had been many times, I wanted to give up on this man. But my love for him would not allow me to even when I wanted to. Ahmad had been my world, and today my world will be complete before God.

I did not look at the bridesmaids and their lavender dresses with a wrap to match. Nor did I look at the groom's men and their white tux with lavender inserts. It was the man in front of me. The slender built man standing six feet and five inches in height, wearing an all-white tux with shoes, hat and a cane to match was the man I had been waiting for.

At that time in my life, Ahmad was my life. I recalled how a part of me wanted to run speedily to him. Soon as my brother gave me the final single hug, he turned to my husband to be and smiled before he sat down. I glanced at my husband to be, and he smiled. When he did, I saw nothing but gold trimmings and eyes that only saw me.

Everything became a blur to me. I remembered our pastor had us turn to each other. Ahmad repeated after

15

*him; then the pastor asked if he had prepared his vows. My
soon-to-be husband faced me. Tears were all upon him as
they streamed gently down his soft, warm face. I reached
up and wiped them away tenderly as he said, "Tygeria, I
have loved you all my life and nothing gives me more
pleasure than knowing in a few minutes we will be united
before God, family, and friends. When I was imperfect and
shut you out, you continued to demonstrate the patience
and love that I needed when I needed it. For that I am
thankful. You have stood by me in more ways than anyone
will ever know and when I thought I was alone you were
still there. Marrying you does not compare to the love I
have for you; it makes me a better man, and it makes us
stronger as a unit. I've had my share of mistakes, but if it
hadn't been for you, I would cease to exist. You are
everything to me and I wouldn't trade you for the world.
You understand me, and you know me and not just that, you
love me for me, which is rare."*

*When he said that my head bowed, my shoulders
crouched as I began to weep silently. Ahmad reached under
my veil, wiped my tears, and said, "When you cry like you
are now, I will be there to wipe every tear that falls from
those beautiful eyes. You will never have to want, and you
will never have to worry if I love you because I will show
you every day the Lord gives me breath to breathe, that I
love you. And as sure as the sun rises in the day and the
moon lights the night, I will love you. I will be there for you
like you deserve, and I would never purposely make you
sad. No woman will ever take your place, and no woman
will ever be in your place because your place is with me in*

my heart."

I began sobbing uncontrollably. I didn't remember saying my vows because I was struck with many emotions that I didn't care what I said. All I knew was I was ready to be his wife and just like that he lifted my veil, and he kissed me like never before. Everyone began to clap as our pastor said, "Church, welcome this union before God and you all, the new lives of Mr. and Mrs. Ahmad Tatum."

We turned to face the people as we held hands. Someone began to clap obnoxiously. Everyone stopped clapping and turned to the middle of the aisle as they began to whisper among themselves. As if it was happening all over again, I felt my hands becoming sweaty as they did at the church. I wiped them on a napkin and began remembering again.

It is here that I looked at my husband and he was not smiling. There on my red carpet was a woman. She was slender inbuilt with a hump in her stomach. I took it that she is with child and about four to five months at that. The worst part was this lady had on a white-looking wedding dress similar to mine but a cheaper version. Quietly I asked my husband with a surprise, "Who is that and why is she wearing a wedding dress at our wedding?"

He didn't respond. He left my side in rage. I lifted my dress and went storming behind him. He made it to her and snatched her arm. The woman then screamed, "Let me go! She needs to know who the real bride is!"

17

As the blades on the ceiling fan cut through the air, the place was just that quiet. I was taken aback by her words. I glanced at Ahmad and yelled with curiosity, "Let her go. Let her go. I want to hear what this woman has to say."

Ahmad looked at me and yelled, "She will not ruin our day with her lies in front of our loved ones!"

Before, I could finish saying, "Why would she ruin my day with lies? Who is she? Why is she here?" He was shaking his head and staring at her.

The woman yelled, "Yeah tell her who am I? Tell that church-going hoe just who I am to you."

During this time, our pastor and J Lamb came over. The pastor said, "Let us go in the study and handle this without the entire church body watching."

With my heart racing at an all-time level high, I lifted up my dress and marched behind Ahmad, with the other three behind me. When I arrived in the large study, Ahmad was pacing the area with his hands on his head saying, "Not like this, oh God help me, not like this."

"Babe, what's going on? What are you talking about, not like this? Who is that woman? Why is she coming here on our wedding day in a white dress? Huh? Tell me."

Ahmad looked more traumatized than anything. I gladly stated to him, "We can overcome any lies. Just tell me so I won't be left in the dark."

From behind the pastor, the cruel woman said, "Tell her babe what's going on so the light can shine on her ass?"

"Who are you?" I screamed at the woman.

She gave me a stupid look with a smile that teased me as she spoke, "Nigeria, because I didn't think he would tell you, I came to make sure he does."

He yelled at her and said, "Shut the hell up B. and her name is Tygeria."

"What the hell ever her name is, she'll be alright. You do what you have to so I can get some cake."

I was shocked. My husband had never show anger like this before. Our pastor, his dad looked at him and said, "Son, calm down. That type of language does not need to be heard in the house of God and explain what is going on?"

Using a softer approach, I asked, "Babe who is she? What is she doing here?"

Calmly he said, "She is the mother to be of my son she carries."

I stepped back as my legs trembled. I could not believe what I just heard so I asked again, "She is who?"

He reached up and touched my fingers as he said,

"She carries my son."

Here I am on my wedding day, not being married a few minutes and already something has taken place. I forgot all about where I was as I slapped him and tried to claw his face off. The preacher tried to get between us but that did not help. J Lamb rushed to me and helped pulled me off his brother.

He must have known her for he said, "It's just like yo bitch ass to fuck up somebody else's life because you fucked yours up. I ought to let Ty go so she can rip that other man's baby out your stomach. Coming up in here destroying a wedding because he won't marry you."

Pain, horror, and confusion swept over me. I didn't know what to think. I couldn't think. I just heard him tell me that another woman is having his baby. I began to panic as those words continued to rack my brain. I could not believe this was happening and when I thought about it, I pretended to ease up, and this time I went for her and my husband shielded her.

Thinking I was mistaken, I went after her again and he protected her again, but this time by pushing me back. What just happened? My facial appearance was that of a misinterpretation of the eyes. I am the wife, and he is the husband, but he stood between me and her. He was protecting her from me as if I were the bad guy.

I don't think I ever cried so hard, but my eyes were cloudy with tears. My mind must have played a trick on my

20

eyes. This could not be the man I just married. Surely not the man I have known all my life has done this evil deed to me. I stopped as I was shocked to see him stopping me from hitting her, pregnant or not; I had to get her.

When she saw that he was blocking me from her she said, "He been cheating on you for months now and your dumb ass didn't have a clue. Eating up all the lies he fed you, even I knew better to eat the shit he put on the plate. Speaking of the plate, there were many times when you called him, you were disturbing him from eating my pussy, talking about messing up a nut."

He turned to her and said, "Shut up. Don't taunt her. You've already done enough."

I never will forget the look as Ahmad stared down at me. He placed his hands on my shoulders. I could not move because I was still thinking about what she just said. My husband of a few minutes spoke in a caring tone, "It's my fault. She has nothing to do with this. If you are going to blame someone blame me. Take your anger out on me. I'm the one that has wronged you, you not her. I can take it. I'm going to be a man about it, Ty. But this does not mean that I don't love you any less."

She said, "Wait a minute. Quit lying to her oversized ass. It's her fault for being fat, chunky, over-weight, thick, or whatever you want to call it. I haven't said anything that you ain't already said about her. You talk about her all the time and if I had a heart, I would have felt sorry for her. Besides, you the one that hates to go home and always saying how she doesn't clean like you want her to. You the one don't want her because her fat ass doesn't turn you on anymore. You the one who said she can't find anybody because she ain't ever had anybody else but you. You said you only gone marry her because you have been with her a long time, and you want to do what is right by that little boy. What you really should have told her is how you say her obese heavy ass stank. Your exact words are in the summer she smells like she's been working with hogs and on a good day, she smells like a sweaty sock in the wind."

Words could not form as I felt like sinking through the floor. Ahmad yelled at her, "Shut up. You can't follow directions? Leave my wife alone."

With power, she said, "Wife? That word's a joke, Ahmad honey. You and I both know that. It was just last night you were with me feeding the baby all night long until you realized that it was getting too late. You vowed to protect me with your life and with every breathe you have. Tell her I'm lying and I'll shut up."

My heart broke when I glared at him as he dropped his head. He came over to me, and I kept pushing him back. I didn't want to hear what he had to say, and I didn't want him to touch me. She stated, "I'm waiting because this bitch needs to know where your heart is really at."

Yelling as loud as I could my words were, "I'm his heart, and I have his son, not you!"

"You ain't never lied girl because fake bitches make

22

me sick," J Lamb said to agree with me.

My brother came to the door and asked, "Ty, you alright in there."

I yelled, "Josh, keep my son with you."

"He's our son" my husband spoke with an authority that I was not listening to as I began to shake my head, no. The pastor said to the woman, "Young lady, leave these two alone. This husband and wife need to talk. They don't need you to provoke matters worse."

"Preacher, if they gone talk, he gone talk in front of me. I'm the real wife."

"You're his bitch and bitches can't be wives," J Lamb said to the woman.

Pastor Tatum raised his voice by saying, "I know tempers are flaring but watch the language we are in the house of God."

They ignored Pastor's words. The woman said, "You don't tell me what the fuck to do. As for you Jamal, call me what the hell you like, but I am the one he keeps coming to, and I mean cum too."

"Ahmad tell yo bitch to leave this bitch alone before this bitch kicks her bitch ass for Ty."

J Lamb and the nameless woman began to argue. Pastor Tatum was trying to calm them down. I looked up and asked Ahmad as calmly as the tone of my voice would *allow me to ask blankly, "She is your wife?"*

"It was not like this, and there isn't any paper trail to say we are legally married. Tygeria believe me, you are my wife. Let me handle this, trust me," Ahmad assured me.

"Trust you?"

She yelled, "He may have married you in front of those people, but he married me in front of God first and according to you Christians, you don't need a paper for that."

Trying to be as calm as I could, I fixed my eyes upon her and said, "He may have done a pretend wedding in front of God, but on earth, the paper is what counts."

Ahmad went over to her and tried removing her from the room. I went after her, and he pushed me back. I thought it was a fluke, so I went after her again. This time like the first time, it was no mistake. He deliberately pushed me down, and when he did, he stared at me with hatred. I was stunned as I got up and went after them both.

He kept me off her as I did my best to get to her as well as hit on him. J Lamb grabbed me, and I scratched him. He glanced back at me for a second. I looked at him humiliated. Ahmad turned around and left with her as J Lamb let me go. I turned around and tried to walk away but fainted.

When I woke up, I was in the hospital, Ahmad was by my side. I sat up and he jumped by me and said with compassion, "You don't need to move so fast, the doctors said you became extremely stressed and passed out."

I didn't say a word. The memory came back as I began to cry all over again.

"Ty, baby, please don't cry baby. You don't need to cry."

"I am not your baby and don't tell me that I don't need to cry! A woman comes to my wedding in a wedding dress and tells me she is having your baby. She said you were just screwing her last night; you took vows in front of God with her first, and you tell me that I don't need to cry."

"It's not how you think it is. Let me explain."

I retorted quickly, "There is nothing to explain. I am a laughingstock in a town that knows all about me now. I have you and her to thank for that."

He began to whimper. I snatched my hand away and turned my nose up at him. He then began pleading, "I know you don't believe me, but I have not stopped loving you."

"You talked about me to her, above all people. You could have told me the truth whenever I would ask you about my weight. You should have told me of your true feelings but you didn't. You could have come to me like a man and told me but instead, you betrayed me with that woman! And I might add that woman will never love nor care for you as I do. She will never do you like a wife

25

should do her husband."

"Ty, when all this came about, I was going through a phase. Mom passed away and you were giving all your attention to Josiah."

"You kidding? You have to be kidding me, right?"

"No, I felt alone. I know he was just a baby, but I was in mourning, and I didn't feel your love. She has been coming after me, and I gave in one night."

"One night or many nights? Tell me."

Dropping his head, he spoke sympathetically "Ty, don't do this."

"Why not? You did. You created an environment that lacks trust and respect; so, don't complain now about the type of atmosphere it is. I thought we were better than this. I never imagined you would stoop low enough to hurt me not just that talk about my weight when you knew that I had been teased enough because I was the new kid at Ackerman."

"For what it is worth, I never wanted this to happen like this. I am sorry I hurt you."

"Hurt is an understatement. You deliberately damaged me, and your actions were intentional. You are a grown man, and you knew what you were doing. There is no excuse."

"It seemed like one at the time, and I am sorry I

ever did it. I made a mistake, and it is one I can't get back."

 "You sorry? You so sorry, but you going to be with her."

 "I didn't say that."

 "You didn't have to. I know because of the way you protected her at the church, and you aren't finished with her. Mark my words, she will be the one to destroy you and when she does, don't expect me to be hanging around."

 It was quiet for the moment as she asked me with watery eyes, "Do you think you will forgive me?"

 That was the day I looked at him in a new light. I stared at him as if he were a stranger. I had been taught that we must forgive if we want our Father in heaven to forgive us. Now I am confronted with this, I am not sure if I will ever forgive him or ever want anything to do with him. Releasing my eyes from him, I said, "Maybe in time but not now. You made my heart love you, and I gave you all of me. When I was faithful and loyal, you took it for granted. When I only saw you, you saw someone else. When the tables turn, tell me who you will see?"

 Ahmad did not answer. He was brought up in the church. He knows what the Word says about reaping what you sow. At that precise moment, he dropped his head, and my brother Josh came in. Ahmad stood up and said, "Let me explain, Josh man."

My brother didn't care what Ahmad had to say. The first thing Josh did was sucker punch my husband in the face. My husband fell back on the small chair. Josh jumped on him, and they began fighting in my room with my brother on top. A nurse heard the rumble and brought in security.

They both were escorted off the property and not allowed to return. I called myself going to sleep. About an hour later Jessica and J Lamb brought my son Josiah in. J Lamb said, "I figured you needed to see some type of joy out of today."

When Josiah said, "Momma" a huge smile crossed my mouth as I broke down as I held onto him. This little guy is all I have now and for some reason, I can't get it together. The past event has made me feel uncertain about a lot of things. J Lamb sat on the edge of my bed to say, "Ty, if I must say so I am so sorry for what my stupid brother has done."

Shaking my head to agree but that did not change the fact that I was hurt. Jessica took Josiah from me and sat beside him when I asked, "How is Josh doing?"

She sighed. "He is in one of those moods where he doesn't want to talk to anyone."

"He has always been like that," I added.

"Ty, I have not ever seen him as upset as he was. Point blank. He was furious at what he heard Ahmad has done. Think about it? He only heard and doesn't know for

28

sure if anything he has heard is of truth. I am so glad security stopped him because you know how protective of you and Josiah your brother can be."

"I know."

Observing J Lamb and Jessica I asked, "Do you any of you know this woman that wrecked my wedding day?"

Jessica spoke first, "I have never heard or seen her before. No one at the wedding knows her because when she was clapping like that, we all were trying to figure out who she was then."

J Lamb gave me that crazy look to say, "Girl, who doesn't know her. She is from here, and she does everyone from here to there."

"So, you do know her?"

"I know her, and it's difficult to explain."

"What is her name?"

"Bianca."

"Yeah, he did say B. I thought he was cutting it short for the real word."

We giggled for a seconds before I asked, "Tell me what you know."

I know excluded herself because she doesn't want any part of it and that's her decision. However, I was stunned a little when J Lamb said, "You might need to ask your husband. And I use the term husband loosely because it's no longer a shacking thing, it's a God thing, and I ain't gone be the one to break that up."

"I don't want to talk to him right now. I don't think I ever want to talk to him, J Lamb. He hurt me and to know he may have a baby on the way."

"You know like I know you have to talk to him. He is Josiah's father and like it or not, your husband."

I began to cry when he said the husband. The doctor came in and told me that I will be able to go home soon as the nurse takes the IV out of my arm tomorrow; they want to make sure there isn't anything else that could have caused me to blackout. When he left, J Lamb said, "We will talk when we get out of here. Plus, I don't think you need to talk in front of your son."

"He's only two."

To make me smile like usual, he said as he laughed "You work with children every day and have five hundred degrees from Psychology, Philosophy, Education, P. E., Jungle Jim, Playground, Kitchen, Bus Driver, Church and Family Counseling. Did I already mention Sociology, too?"

That was too funny. I laughed for the first time since my life changed. J Lamb spoke, "Whatever it is in, I'm sure you have that covered. But have you forgotten how smart children at his age are? He can pick up the slightest thing if anything is wrong."

A smile creased my lips as I laughed a little more.

"That is the Ty I know. Don't let this get to you and don't let what she and he did get to you. You are my girl, and you are better than that. You are a strong, independent, classy woman that takes care of herself."

"J Lamb, I don't know."

"Yeah, you do. You believe in your God, and you have faith. Make that your top priority and watch how your life will change. Also, if you add a little make-up and show some breast from time to time, you will be alright."

"Tell your brother to move out. I don't want to talk to him or see him right now."

"I will tell him, and I will tell him to do it so he can give you time to adjust to all that happened. I am sure he will do it because he loves you."

"If this is love, show me hate."

CHAPTER 2

J Lamb looked at me. I needed that but I feel like I need to be alone. Today is supposed to have been the happiest day of my life, but I was in a hospital and married to a man that has another family. My best friend J Lamb won't tell me, but if I know him as I do, he will tell me when he thinks I am calm enough to handle it.

I looked over at Jessica and asked, "Can Josiah stay at y'all house? When I get out, I will come by and get him."

"Ty, we love having him at our house. You know it is never a problem."

"I know, but you are his wife, and I have to do things in order."

"I understand, and I am thankful for your consideration. He can stay with us for a while until you get it together. I mean that way you won't be stressing."

"Thanks, Jessica. Bring him here; let me kiss him good night."

She hands my son back to me, and I didn't want to let him go. I know I have loose ends to tie up; I can't do it like I want to if he is here. Jessica and Josh will take great care of him until I come get him, that much I am sure, but I need my son near me; he is all I have now. Soon as my sister-in-law left with my son, a million thoughts crossed my mind.

J Lamb tapped my foot and asked, "What you thinking about?

"You know me all too well."

"I am your best friend in the world."

"Don't forget to tell your brother to get out of the apartment."

"You only been married for what? A few hours and already you kicking him out? Bitch!"

A grin replaced my frown as I responded, "Just tell him."

"I'll tell him. I'll do better than that. I will tell him so you can listen, just be quiet."

J Lamb dialed Ahmad's phone. He answered on the first ring, "J Lamb, how is she doing?"

Just hearing his voice made me muffle my cry. He sounded so sincere about my well-being, but it still does not change the detail that he cheated on me with a woman like that. J Lamb looked over at me to warn me to be quiet as he said, "I don't know how she is doing. You should know she is your wife not mine."

"If her brother hadn't come in and started a fight, I would be there with her now."

"What makes you so sure, he started it, or you will be here with her? You made her look like a laughingstock

in front of everyone."

"Just tell her I love her."

"Man Ahmad, I ain't telling her that. You done fucked up and you want me to tell her something you don't mean."

"J Lamb, you know I love her. Ty means the world to me."

"What world you in? Can't be the one we live in because the last time I checked love don't hurt. Let me ask her?"

J Lamb yelled at me, "Ty does love hurt?"

Not giving me a chance to respond, he got back on the line to Ahmad and said, "She said no, love doesn't hurt."

"I don't care what y'all say. I know who I love."

"Then what you called today letting that trashy-home-wrecker come to your wedding and destroy the only real thing you could have had with my girl?"

"It wasn't supposed to be like that."

"Well, it happened like that supposed to or not."

J Lamb looked at me. I turned my head and took my index finger to make circles for J Lamb to wrap up the conversation. He got the message and said, "Well, I was calling on her behalf because she wants you to move out."

34

The line was quiet, and he said it again, "You hear me?"

"Yeah, I heard you."

"Well, get your shit and get on down. You took up space long enough."

"She didn't say that like that. I know she didn't."

"I did say I was speaking on her behalf so I can put her words in any order I want as long as you get the message."

"She wants me to move out so fast, huh?"

"Don't tell me you thought she was going to still live in the house with your cheating ass? She probably can't trust you to check the mail. I wouldn't because I know me."

"It wasn't like that. Why everyone thinks I was doing it like that? You know me, J Lamb."

"Ahmad, I know you cheated. It may not have been like that, but she is pregnant. She said y'all took vows in front of God first. If my memory serves me right, you know that is the most important thang, for y'all Christians. Anyway, are you gone move out or what? I need to know what to tell her, while you on my phone wasting my minutes that you hate to buy."

"Tell her I want to talk to her, and I won't leave until she talks to me."

35

He looked over at me with questions on my face as to what to say now. I shook my head, no. J Lamb said, "I told her, and she doesn't want to be in the room with you; the smell of lies and skunks makes her sick. Hell, it makes me sick."

I laughed at that because J Lamb always knows how to make a bad situation look a little better. Ahmad stated, "All those things she said were taken out of context. I did not say it the way she said I did."

"Ahmad, you had no business talking about your main lady to an outside hoe, even I know better than that with my hoes. You might as well move out so she can move on."

Ahmad was quiet for a few minutes then he said in quietness, "Tell her I'll move out, and I'll be gone when she gets here. I won't take anything but my clothes."

It actually hurt me in part to hear him say he would move out. I thought he would have put up a fight, but he in his usual tone said he'll be gone. Every waking moment of the past eleven years of my life was with him in some form. Even to a fourteen-year-old girl, I knew then he was the one for me, just like I know now.

I snapped back just in time to hear J Lamb say, "You could put up a fight to assure her of your love. You leave with your tail tucked between your legs, just like that."

"I've already caused her so much pain. If she doesn't want to see me, I will wait until she wants to see

36

me, then she and I can talk like adults."

"Well, I don't know how long that will be. You did have another woman come to her soon as the people were welcoming you and her as husband and wife."

"I am willing to wait for her; I love her."

"Go get your stuff out, and I will let her know what you said."

"Tell her I love her, and I meant my vows."

I began to cry out loud. He heard me as he said, "Ty, baby."

J Lamb hung up. He looked at me and said, "I know you didn't want to hear him say that, so I shut it down for you. Honestly, I didn't want to hear it."

"Thanks, I appreciate it."

Another knock was heard, and we looked at each other. I then spoke, "Come in."

It was my father-in-law, the preacher. J Lamb looked at me and said, "Well, this is my cue to leave."

"Jamal, you don't have to leave," Pastor Tatum said to his son.

"Daddy, you about to do some counseling and talk about church, so, yes, I do have to leave."

"Ok, but you are welcomed to stay."

37

Jamal gave me a hug and said, "Girl, I'll stay at your place tonight to make sure he doesn't take any stuff that doesn't belong to him."

"You mean, so you can ramble through my stuff after he leaves."

With laughter, he spoke candidly, "Yeah, girl, that too."

He left out and Pastor Tatum sat down beside me. I turned my head for tears were streaming delicately down my cheeks.

"It's okay, Tygeria. Let it out. Crying is good for the soul, and the Lord bottles our tears."

I snap back to reality and wiped my eyes again. The pain is still fresh as it was yesterday. I know that being gone wouldn't cure me completely, but I had to try. I took a deep breath and started back recalling my past when the preacher came to visit me.

I cried for what seemed like hours, and my pastor was there to comfort me. Nothing I could think of could make me feel better, not even the thoughts of my son. Today I was being self-centered because no bride is supposed to be feeling like this after marrying the man of her dreams, but I was.

The more I thought about Ahmad and that woman, I cried. The more I thought about how he talks about me to her, I cried. Just the thought of knowing that he was with

38

her just last night and how he kept me in the dark, I cried. At this point, I didn't want any cheering up, and I didn't want to think about it. All I wanted was to sleep.

Somewhere amid in the crying, I did fall asleep. When I opened my eyes, my father-in-law was still there. He smiled and said, "The nurse came in and gave you a shot. You were crying so much. Tygeria, you were doing physical damage on your body, so she gave you something to help you rest."

"Please give me some water."

He got up and poured me some water in the cup and handed it to me. I sat up in bed and sipped the water.

"Thank you."

He placed the cup on the stand and said, "I know you don't want to talk about what you are going through, but it is now when the enemy will place un-rebuked thoughts in your mind. Right now, you are grieving and don't want to talk, but I tell you now is the time you need to talk."

"I agree."

Pastor Tatum prayed, "Lord allow me to say something to reach your daughter. She has been wronged and needs clarity. Grant her such and open her for forgiveness and wisdom. Deal with her mind and heart as well as her husband's. Let them know that you work through all situations and only you know the purpose. In your precious name Jesus, Amen."

"Amen."

"Now, I want to tell you I am sorry, and you must not let this harden your heart. Damage has already been done, but it does not mean you are at the end, and you can grow from what you have been through."

"I will forgive him in time but not now. I just can't."

"I know not now but I pray it's soon. I know you both can work this out and still have a productive marriage. It can be done."

"Pastor, a man did not come to your wedding wearing a tux and stating the things she stated to me. Your wife did not become pregnant by another man."

He was quiet as if he were debating on something in his head. He said, "A man may not have come to my wedding dressed in a tux, but yes, my wife has placed me in a situation similar to yours."

I stopped talking. I never knew that, and I knew his wife years before she recently passed away.

"Tygeria let me tell you, my story. My wife and I were very much like you, but the difference was I ran from the call on my life. She simply embraced it. At that time, Ahmad was one, and she was going through a period of depression and rejection. It wasn't until I played too long, and she became pregnant by another man, from another church. She could have passed Jamal off as mine, but she

didn't. She told me, and you talking about crying. I was furious and upset. I wanted to kill them, seek revenge. How my church-going wife could slip and have a baby by another man, I didn't know? I asked so many questions and finally the answer came. While I was out being me, being a man she sought comfort in another man. She had made me her business, but when I told her to get out of my business, she found business elsewhere. I didn't realize all those times she was on my back she was making me be a better man. From that news, I went after comfort in women, booze, and illegal drugs. None of this helped me. I didn't care and parts of me didn't want to live. One day when I was high and dying in my urine, an angel visited me. He told me that if I didn't snap out and run for the Lord, I was going to die and go to hell right then and there. You talk about someone getting their act together. I asked her to forgive me, and she was confused when she was the one that transgressed. I told her that if I had been the man she needed, she would not have needed another man. We went to our pastor and had counseling. I admit sometimes it was hard to look at Jamal for it reminded me of his mother's one-time affair, but God delivered me from that. I know what my son did was wrong, and how he should have told you, but he didn't. You, he, nor I can change what happened, but you can learn from it and go on."

"Is this when you gave your life to Christ?"

He gave me a pause then spoke, "It is, but it took time to come full circle."

41

"Do they know?"

"Yeah, they know, but that didn't stop them from being as close as they are now. I love them both the same and to me, they both are my boys. Jamal calls me dad, and for that God is the reason why I never made difference in them."

"Pastor, I have always been good and from this point being good has only hurt me."

"That is not so. The enemy wants to make it look like that but being good has advantages and right now you are very hurt. You can't focus on the good because right now, you only see the bad that has happened."

"I'm troubled, depressed, confused and so tired of crying. I want this pain to stop ripping at my heart."

"The word tells us to cast our cares upon the Lord, for He cares for us. Tell Jesus all about your problems and let him do it because if you do it, you will only make a mess."

"That's just it. I did all I could do, and this is the thanks I got."

"Tygeria, you are like many women, you do your best and that is all you can do. That is all Christ is asking any of us to do. He knows the flesh is weak and needs him but if you let him, he will heal your hurt."

"I have loved Ahmad since I was fourteen and to

love a man that long and not see his lies is shattering. He played me some kind of stupid and how could I have not known, he was doing this to me?"

"You can't see what you don't want to see, and you can't see what he doesn't want you to see. You trusted him with your whole heart, and he placed that love and trust in the wrong thing, which was the flesh. Ever since the passing of his mother, my son changed. You know yourself that he became distant. Right now, Ahmad needs time to sort out the mess he has gotten in, just like you. You both are going to have to talk and must make a decision if this marriage is what you want. And if it is, there will be a lot of man-hours placed in it and a lot of insecurities on both ends."

"How is that when he is the one that hurt me?"

"Because you remained faithful, he is going to think that you will do to him what he did to you."

"Pastor, that is far from the truth. I am not him. I love him and right now, I still love him. My heart still beats for him just a little slower that's all."

"It will take time, but you both can live and move on from this if you choose to. You both must come to terms, if not for you both, but your son."

"How can I ever trust him again?"

"That is something only you and God will know. You may not ever trust him to the fullness, but you can be

43

able to trust him again. You both must be willing to do what you have to because of this breach."

"Right now, I'm actually still shocked."

"So am I, but you can't continue to dwell on it. You must continue to praise God amid during in this storm and believe me, storms don't last always; the sun will shine."

With a faint smile, I added, "Well the sun needs to come on out. I don't like the rain."

"I wish it was that fast. God does things on his time, and it can be speedily."

There was a long pause before he said, "I'm going to go now. I hope I said something to help. He is still legally your husband, and no one will look down on you for taking him back and you both going on from this. Make sure whatever decision you make, it's a decision you will live with and not regret."

Shaking my head slowly, I spoke softly and sorrowfully, "I know."

Standing to his feet, Pastor Tatum spoke with ease to me, "Get some rest and do some soul searching before you make a rash decision that will affect the rest of your life."

"I will. Bye Pastor."

"Bye, Tygeria."

He left out the door and I was alone once again, with my thoughts. I closed my eyes and began to sleep. For the first part of the night, I could hear the words and see the deceit being played out right before my eyes. I even awoke in tears and longing for Ahmad to be here for me, but he wasn't. The more I slept, the more I cried. It was like something taking over the water in my body and making me cry for hours.

Nothing was working. I even prayed but I still cried. I even got up and read scriptures, which, helped until I closed the book to close my eyes. All night all I could hear were bible verses to comfort my broken heart and all I could see was the taunting in this woman's voice but that did not bother me as much.

The one thing that hurt so bad was the fact that he was protecting her. He will say he wasn't, but most men do that for women they care without knowing it. But I witnessed it with my own eyes. Ahmad was not letting any harm come to the woman that ruined my wedding day. To him, it appeared okay, for her to do so because he would not let me near her. When I am his wife and the one, he just poured his heart out to in front of God, family, and friends.

How could this woman have so much power over him and yet destroy him, without him having a clue? Questions like that puzzled me all night. Doesn't she know that God is going to get her for breaking up a marriage or causing problems in marriage; even though, he may have pursued her? It's like morals don't exist in this world and women

45

think they have more rule over wives.

I thought about Ahmad when that statement crossed my mind. I must come to terms with him being with me or without me. I either want him back or I don't. I just can't let the man I love to walk out on me. I thought about that and this time, I went to sleep happier than ever.

The next morning, I awoke and called J Lamb to come to get me before he left for work at the Winston County Medical Center. He came and the first thing he said was, "You look revived. What daddy do, soak you in the hospital tub filled with Olive Oil to cast the devil out you?"

I laughed and responded by saying, "No he talked to me, and I received it."

"Let me guess, you going to work it out with Ahmad?"

"I'm going to try at least that is the plan right now."

"Well, he is your husband, go get him."

"Let me use your phone, I want to call him."

As I dialed his number, J Lamb asked "Where you want me to take you? You know I can't be late for work."

"You already late and take me to the apartment."

Ahmad picked up and I said, "Hey."

He was quiet then he said, "Hey how are you doing?"

"Well as expected. How about yourself?"

I was quiet as he asked, "You out the hospital?"

"Yeah, I just got out. J Lamb is taking me back to Ackerman as we speak. Why you not at work?"

"Today is Sunday."

"Yeah, it is, isn't it?"

Another awkward silence. Ahmad said slowly, "I got my clothes out yesterday as you wanted. I also paid the rent for the next month for you. You don't have to move off Seward Street, it's a good area for Josiah to live at."

Bypassing what he was saying I asked, "Where you at, maybe we can talk?"

"Now is not a good time."

"Where are you living at?"

"I'm staying with one of my co-workers."

"Where bout? Maybe I can swing by and see you."

"That is not good. You need to go home and rest. You did just get out of the hospital."

"I didn't have surgery. I was stressed but you acting like you don't want to talk to me. Are you whispering?"

"I'm not whispering."

"Then speak up, I can barely hear you."

To rush me he spoke, "I will come by and see you."

"Where you at?"

"I told you I'm at one of my co-workers, why? You told me to get out, remember?"

"You at her house, aren't you?"

"No. If you calling to talk about her; I'll talk to you later because I don't want to discuss her when I talk to you."

"Fine, I just made it home. What time are you coming?"

"In another hour or so."

"Ok, love you."

"Yeah."

When I hung up, I said, "He didn't tell me he loved me. He only said, yeah."

"Ty, you no fool; he's at her house, he has to be."

"Where she lives?"

"Wait a minute, private investigator. You not about to get me jail time for stalking and instigating nothing. I *can't go to prison. Wait, I might can."*

"I'm being serious. If you don't want in and don't like drama, I understand you not the same J Lamb you used to be."

"I didn't say that, but you married and that is a whole new level."

"What does that mean?"

"It means I am being late for work."

I got out of the car and unlocked the door by using the spare from under the mat. When I walked in, I sat on the couch. Instantly, it all hit me. I started back crying. Never had I experienced such a heartbreak like now. I kept hearing her say, you fat and he's not turned on by you any more of how he says I stank. There is no telling what else he has said to her about me. This is all so unreal to me and to know, my Ahmad feels like that angered me more than hurt me.

My cell rang and it was Josh, my brother. I cleared my voice by answering. A bright and cheerful tone said, "Hey, Ty, how are you doing?"

"I'm okay. J Lamb just dropped me off. Is Josiah ok?"

"He's good. I want you to be the first to know that Jessica is having a baby."

I screamed because if anyone deserves a baby more,

49

it's the two. They have been wanting a family for as long as I can remember and they have been together even longer. I know they are going to make great parents. Trying not to yell so, I exclaimed "Congrats to you and Jessica. I am so happy for you guys."

"Me, too. At first, I thought she was just playing but she showed me the test, and I nearly jumped out of my skin."

We laughed because we know it must be something mighty powerful to make my brother show any emotions. I asked, "When is she going to the doctor for a more positive due date?"

"She gonna go in the morning when the health department opens up. She thinks she is about six weeks or so but don't know."

"You need me to come to get Josiah?"

"No. She wants to keep him a little longer. I guess to practice on him."

"Well, that is fine with me. I need to think clearly."

The phones became silent, for I knew he wants to ask me what I was going to do. Beating him to the punch I said, "I'm going to talk to Ahmad, and hopefully we decide to work this out."

Josh was even quieter as I said, "You hear me?"

He spoke, "Tygeria Homely-Tatum, you are a married

woman now. You have to do what is best for you and your son, but personally, I don't trust him anymore. He hurt you and for that he hurt me, and I don't like to be hurt."

"Josh, let me handle it. I know you are only being protective of me, but I need to do this for my new family."

"I know you do. I just hate liars and thieves. He lied to you and stole your heart in the process."

"But he is still my husband," I added.

"I know that I just hate that."

"Let me get off the phone and get settled. I appreciate you bringing my car home and keeping Josiah a little bit longer."

"You're family and that is why I am here to help you in any way I can."

"Love you, Josh."

"Love you, too, Ty, bye."

I went straightaway to shower. The water felt great on my skin as I cleaned myself up. I text my boss and told her that I would be out for a few more days. I am sure she knows because she lives in Louisville, and everybody knows everything. She only text back take your time; when she said that she let me know then, she knows.

"I wonder how work is going to go," I said out loud as I put on my comfortable clothes. I didn't want to put on

51

anything sexy because of the hurtful things she said he said about me. Seconds later the doorbell rung and it was Ahmad. I said, "Come in."

He came in looking as gorgeous as ever. He always had a way of making me smile. I said, "Sit down."

"I can't stay long I have someone out there in the car waiting on me."

I stood up like the devil touched by Holy oil. I asked, "Who waiting on you?" as I peep out the blind. There in his car was the woman from my wedding. I flexed the blind back in haste, and he shook his head as he looked at the floor.

Realizing it was a bad idea he turned his head and said, "I'll come back later."

He reached for the doorknob, but I was there quicker. I blocked the door and said, "No, you not going anywhere."

"Ty, move."

"So, you living with her?"

"Ty, move."

"Wait, tell me. Are you living with her, yes or no simple as that?"

Sternly and unlike him, he replied "I will be back."

"Answer the question! Are you living with her,

answer me?" I yelled.

Almost raising his voice, Ahmad stated "No, I live with a co-worker"

"You not leaving this apartment. I want her ass to come in here so I can flow her ass for trespassing."

"Ty, you cursing now? She pregnant and you don't need to be fighting."

"You don't come in here and tell me what I need to do and not do. If I want to swear, I will do just that!"

"Move Ty, let me out."

"No! You not going anywhere until we talk."

"I'm not talking but you better move from in front of the door."

I continued to stand my ground, and he began pulling me out the way. We began tussling; something we have never done before in this manner. He was pulling me and ripping my clothes. I didn't care. I wasn't going to let him leave. He never should have brought her to my house, but he did.

Yelling all kinds of hurtful things crossed my mind so I said, "What, she doesn't trust you? I did."

He would not answer. He kept trying to move me from the door. Finally, he grabbed my throat and squeezed. I took it as long as I could. He let me go and said, "You need

53

to sit your big ass down somewhere. I said I will be back."

"Don't you ever bring her back here again!"

"Don't worry, I won't."

He opened my door and slammed it. I cried for a second, then ran out behind him. He saw me coming and put the car in reverse. He wasn't fast enough. I picked up a brick from the ground and threw it at his car. The shattering of the backside glass made a loud sound. He hit the brakes and got out. He looked at me and yelled, "I know you didn't just bust my window out!"

Ahmad was angry, and I can tell it in his words. He has never been like this before, so this was new to me. He charged towards me. I ran back into the house and locked the door. He kept acting like he was trying to get in by hitting the door on numerous tries. He gave up for people were looking and he knows they will call the police. He sped off, and I sat on the couch numb and dazed. I didn't have the courage, heart, or guts to talk to anyone. I couldn't. The best day of my life has turned into a nightmare, and the more I thought about the events that have occurred the more I hated myself for being gullible, inexperienced, and unlearned when it comes to love and my heart.

CHAPTER 3

For the next few days, I did not talk to anyone. I didn't want to pray or read God's Word. I didn't even call to check on my son or talk to J Lamb. When people did call, the voicemail picks it up. I am in my own world and in here I feel safe from pain. Sleeping was not any better and discovering pm pills did wonders for me at night. When I awake, I cried and when I went to sleep, I cried.

It seems like all I do is cry. My eyes ached from all the crying I did, and my head would not let me rest for long. This cycle I am in seems to revolve around Ahmad and Bianca. My every thought was of him and how he is happy without me. I was doing more damage to myself than good, but when you are sad you are sad.

Even when my brother texts me, I was reluctant to answer, but he does have my son. I then called him and said, "Hello."

"Ty, what's going on with you? I haven't heard from you, and I was getting worried."

"I'm okay."

"How are you okay, when you haven't been at work, and no one knows where you are?"

"I'm here at home."

"Lil sis, I love you and I know you weren't dealt a

55

fair hand, but life is like that. We shake ourselves off and get back up."

"He is my husband."

"Yes, he is a husband to a wife that is drowning in sorrow and self-pity."

We both were quiet when he said, "I'm sorry but you needed to hear it."

"Yeah."

"Come on Ty. It's going to be okay."

"Yeah."

My brother knows when I keep my answers short it means I don't want to discuss what we are talking about. He asked, "Why won't you come over for a late dinner?"

"I might."

"You need to surround yourself with people who love you."

"I know."

We were quiet again as I said, "Do you want to know what she said to me in the study area of the church?"

"I don't want to know if you don't want to tell me."

"She said, Ahmad calls me fat behind my back and hates to come home to me."

My brother was quiet. I had been teased some for being overweight all my days. When I met J Lamb and Ahmad, I was no longer teased. They took me under their wings, and we all became the best of friends, but Ahmad and I fell for each other. Josh said, "Ty, don't give in to what one person says another says."

"Josh, it came from him because when she said it he dropped his head. Not just that, she said he says I smell like I work with hogs all day and a jockey sock in the wind."

Josh did not speak. I know he was getting angry because I had extensive counseling at Community Counseling for the depression and withdrawals. The black children did the most damage, and I only assumed it was because I moved there after the death of our parents. A hint of sadness was in my speech as I said, "I'm okay, Josh."

He still did not say another word as I tried to assure him, "I am fine. I'm just tired. So much has happened in my life, and I need to get a grip that is all."

"Ty, I want that bastard to pay for what he has done to you and Josiah."

"Josh, he will, but in time and on God's time."

"That is true. Sometimes I want to scream because I tried to protect you from the heartache, but I failed."

"You did a great job in raising me and for that, I am blessed. I have a great son by the way, how is he

doing?"

"He's doing great."

"What the doctor say about Jessica?"

"She is pregnant and due within seven months or so, just like she thought."

"I'm going to be an aunt, and now I have to work on how to spoil it if it's a girl."

"You have a long time to figure it out. Right now, I need you to smile and listen to what the Lord tells you."

"I am going to smile and I will listen."

"Okay. I look forward to seeing you sometime today."

If I hadn't sounded like I was doing better, Josh would have done something that would have landed him in jail or worse. I don't need him in trouble for my battles. The truth be known is, I was afraid to stick my head out the door for people may remember that day I busted the window out, and I know they haven't forgotten my wedding.

I'm quite sure I am the talk of the town because she is not from here. I even looked on Facebook and none of my friends said anything, but I did notice that Ahmad had changed his relationship status from married to in a relationship. I dropped my iPhone and cried like a newborn baby.

I got a text from J Lamb. It read: Girl, I know you sulking in that apartment, but you need to snap out of it. What's for you is for you and if it's not hell with it.

I decided to call him, so I said, "Hi."

"Girl, you one person no one has seen."

Slowly I spoke, "I am staying out of sight and out of mind."

"That only works in the movies, and this is real life."

I laughed a few seconds then he said, "I'm going to help you out."

"How are you going to do that?"

"Put on some clothes, and I will pick you up in a few."

I hung up and put on some baggy clothes. I didn't feel like going anywhere. I even told my boss that I was sick and needed another week off from work. If I keep this up, I will be moving because I can't pay for this apartment and any other bills.

Right before J Lamb came I called the bank and saw that almost all our money was gone. When it used to be five thousand only a thousand was left. I didn't want to cry for I was tired of doing that. I finally sat there in dismay. J Lamb pulled up as I locked the door as I came out. Upon opening the door I said, "Take me to Wal-Mart. I need to swipe a card."

"Which Wal-Mart?"

"It doesn't matter."

"I'll take you to the Ville since it is on our way."

"Okay."

"Girl, how you get the money? You ain't got paid yet. You ain't even been back to work. You quit or something?"

"I haven't quit but if I did, you gone take care of us?"

"If I take care of you, who will take care of us? I barely make a living myself."

We laughed at that as I said, "I know but if I don't get the rest of my money out of the bank, I will be broke."

"Dang, you mean she done hypnotized that nigga to the point where he is taking y'all money?"

"I don't know what you want to call it, but we had five thousand, now there is only one grand left."

J Lamb pulled off as he said, "She got my brother voodoo or something. He ain't never done anything like that before."

"J Lamb, I have to find out who she is and where she lives."

60

"That's what I am here for. I thought about what you said the other day about how I don't like drama anymore. I came here to remind you that drama is a part of my name. Brother or not, he is a cheater, and he did some foul shit to my girl."

I did not say a word. We left out the gates and drove toward Louisville. Quickly I remembered that he said the Wal-Mart is on our way; so, I asked, "She from Louisville?"

"I said she from here and does everybody from everywhere when you were at Winston Medical Center Hospital."

"Which part?"

"Girl, you act like I know that town like that."

"You know enough about it, that much I do know."

"I don't know what you call this part but from what I know she a bad bitch in the bed you hear me. Shit, she a bitch after my own heart because she is known for making men leave home, like my brother."

Cutting my eyes at him he said, "Sorry girl but hell it is the truth. His dumb ass left a good bitch for a bad bitch."

"She might be."

He drove a little bit farther until we entered the Winston County line. He then said, "Tiger, I had nothing to do with it."

61

"I know you didn't."

"I knew her before Ahmad did and I didn't know my brother was caught like that. Ahmad won't tell me anything because he knows I will tell you. I'll squeal like a pig seeing a knife."

"So far you haven't told me anything."

"See, that is why I am making it up to you."

"Do you know her?"

"I know of her, and you wouldn't believe how."

"But you haven't given me her name or anything."

"Her name is Bianca T. Charleston better known as Bitch."

Raking my brain, I said, "I have never heard of her."

"Why would you? We live in Ackerman, and we don't get down in the A-town, as they do there. Wait, I lied we just don't publicize it. We keep it down low."

He drove a few more minutes to say, "I don't know the whole story about her and my brother, but I do know I could not give you half-answers because I know me."

We were quiet for a few more moments as we approached the four-way stop. J Lamb looked at me and said, "I know Ahmad is your husband, but if you going to get out, I won't take you. I need you to stay in the car and watch."

"Why are you doing this? I mean we have been best friends forever, and Ahmad has been there as well. He is your brother, and I am just an outsider."

"I will tell you when you come out."

He turned into Wal-Mart, and I got out. When I came out, I had all the cash to my name in my pocket. I thought if she gets the money, she is good but when I got in the car, J Lamb said, "Blood does not make us family, being there for each other does. He is my brother, but you are just more important as a sister to me than any trick he could ever bring home. I am for right and by law, he is rightfully your husband, and you are my new sister. So, are you ready to see where she lives?"

"Yeah."

We left out of Wal-Mart and pulled into this community by Wal-Mart. It was nice. Every car we saw was a 2010 or better. I looked at him and said, "She lives over here in these nice-looking houses?"

"Girl, it is still the projects."

"It doesn't look like it to me."

"But it is, and she lives there for free because her dad owns half of the good-looking projects around here."

"So, it's a money thing?"

"No, it's a bitch thing. Just because she could not have him she went after him until he gave in. From my reports, all this happened when Momma died."

"He did change when that happened."

"She went after him, and he slept with her. From that point on they were messing around more off than on."

Just that knowledge alone achse me. My best friend said, "I know it hurts you to hear this but it's all out now. It's best to hear it all now than to hear stuff later after you were beginning to heal."

"You right."

"When he decided to marry you, he backed off her, but she was pregnant and screaming it's his. I don't think it's his. On the other hand, Josiah is his. He already has big feet and looking like he's ten years old."

Laughter filled the car as he drove a few more feet.

"He is not that tall."

"Close enough. Look at him? Looks like Ahmad spit him out himself."

He stopped his car in front of this apartment house. I looked at him and he asked, "You see anything?"

"No, why?"

"Look again but this time look behind us in the

mirror."

My heart was pounding loudly as I saw Ahmad come out of this apartment from the back of us. A guy came out and J Lamb said, "That's his co-worker who happens to be her brother. So technically, he does stay with his co-worker, but he didn't add she lived there too."

I felt J Lamb staring at me as I saw my husband get into that guy's pretty Camaro.

"That's Blackie her brother. I don't know why he even works. He has money and hoes lined up for days just to get with him, but he doesn't chase them."

Dropping my head, I thought verbally, "Where have I seen him before?"

"Tiger, he came over one day, and he said he liked the way you cooked that chicken on a stick."

"Sure did. Since that day, Ahmad never brought him back over and that was a long time ago."

"Look a there," J Lamb said with anger.

Ahmad and her brother weren't gone but a few minutes when another man pulled up. He got out and went inside. We grinned at each other as we both knew that she was seeing another man. J Lamb smiled so hard that he said, "Now that's a bitch for real. She broke up that nigga home and still doing her thing. He gonna flip out when he finds out, and I ain't telling him."

"I'm not either, but how do we know that it's another man? It could be a friend."

He looked at me sideways to say, "That's what I don't like about you. You always look on the brighter side, which is good, but today it doesn't work. That is a nigga she seeing and Ahmad is stupid. I know it, and you know it. Call it for what it is."

We sat there stalking their apartment for another hour and finally the guy came out. She walked him to the car, and they kissed. J Lamb cut his eyes at me and said, "Hmmmmm, what I tell you?"

"You right."

The car Ahmad was in, and the other guy's car had to past each other because a few seconds later he and Blackie pulled back up. Ahmad said something to Blackie, and then he headed towards us.

"Oh, shit he coming, Tiger," J Lamb said as I tried to slump down in the seat.

Ahmad knocked on my window, and J Lamb let it down, and said to me, "What he ain't busting my window out."

"Ty, what you doing here?"

"I had to see if you lived with her."

He looked over at his brother and said, "I should have known."

66

"What, Ahmad?"

"J Lamb, don't what me."

"I see you are the happy family man without me and Josiah," I said as he glanced back at me.

"Ty, not now, and it's not like that. I have to find out what it is I want."

"How you going to do that if you not going to church and you still having sex with her, while I am seeing no one."

"It's complicated."

J Lamb butted in to say, "How complicated is it if you getting your groove on and she isn't? I mean I am no rocket scientist, but if you put a baking soda with vinegar it will explode."

Trying to throw his weight, Ahmad said to his brother "Take her home."

"Home is where the heart is, so where is your home?" I asked.

"Goodbye Ty, and don't come back. If you do, I will press charges for the window you broke. You lucky I don't do anything about it right now."

J Lamb looked at me, crank up the car to say, "Tiger, shut up and, Ahmad, you don't have to repeat it."

Ahmad backs up from the car, and J Lamb pulled out. I looked at him and said, "You coward."

"No, the hell I ain't. He not about to tear up my shit, because of yo shit. Ain't nobody gonna repair this car but me. If anybody gonna tear this up, it will be me and not that fool you married. Plus, I don't have insurance."

We rode in silence until we reached the Choctaw County line. I asked, "J Lamb, you are my other best friend in the entire world. What do I need to do?"

"What daddy tell you?"

"I tried but my husband won't talk to me. It's like he wants me to wait while he figures out whatever it is he is seeking. I can't, and I refuse to put my life on hold just because he is torn."

"You will be silly if you do, then yet again I am telling you from a world point of view."

"How is it that you act worldly but gives me advice from a biblical point of view?"

"It's because I know to do but won't do. I am not ready to give up the way I live, even though, I have been taught better all my life. I know when God is intervening and when it is man. I just like being me without the heavy consequences church folks put on you but that doesn't mean I don't pray and believe God can do anything and everything but fail."

"How about your dad?"

"You know Pastor Tatum is not my dad. My mom never told me who my dad was, and I didn't care because Pastor Tatum raised me, and I have his last name. To me, he is my dad and that is good enough for me."

"You right. Whoever raises you is your parent, not the one that made you because anyone can make a baby."

I did not say anything more. I have to get on my grind and think but I can't. I am hurting and feel that I can't go on without my husband. J Lamb put me out at home, and I went inside. Soon as he left, I got in my car and went to get Josiah. It wasn't late, but I told my brother that I will bring him back in the morning.

Josh placed my son in his car seat, and we left. I headed back towards Louisville. I went straight to our church. When I arrived, no one was there. I turned the lights off and looked back at Josiah. He was asleep. I wept and got out of the car. I have to do it, or I won't do it. Unlocking the doors, I went in and turned the podium lights on at the altar.

I sat down and looked back and painfully remembered that hurtful day. As much as I tried to get over it, I couldn't. After tonight, I realized that the only man I have loved, loves me no longer. It hurts and it pain me in a way I never thought I would experience. With shaking hands, I sat at the altar with my back to the podium as if it were the preacher in my mind.

As clear as day, everything flooded back. I was fat, worthless, and good for nothing. The one thing I loved the most has been slandering my name to this other woman and to top it off, she told me in front of my best friend and my pastor. My head bowed as I sobbed the tears onto my skirt. Verbally I announced loudly, "God, why you do this to me! I have prayed and fast for an answer, but you have not spoken to me. Why did the man I love choose a woman like that over your daughter! Why! God, why! Am I being punished for shacking? Am I disobedient in some areas and don't know? Haven't I lived the way you wanted me to? Haven't I served you with my whole heart? Then tell me what else is left for me? Oh, God, help me. I have nothing and no one to love me. I don't know what to do. I am at the end of my rope, and if you don't help me, I will do what I came here to do."

Tears came down like a waterfall and my head began to pain me. The more I reminisced on that day, the more I cried as I fell to my knees and squalled. Still, nothing and I just cried my heart out to God. The pains are still here but stronger. I tried drying my tears but at this point that no longer mattered. I picked up the gun and closed my eyes.

When I opened my mouth, I heard a sleepy tone say, "Ma, what you do?"

Those were the words coming from my son. I did not want him to see me do this because I did not want him to have this memory in his mind in any form. My son coming in accurately stopped me. I had to wipe away the tears because I still could not see.

Soon as I did, I saw my son standing there staring at me as he wiped his eyes from his nap. It never occurred to me that I was being selfish in taking my own life; all I wanted was the pain to stop. I came to a low point in my life only thinking about me and the heartache his father had given me.

How I was robbing my son out of a mother did not matter. How I was going to make my brother be the only family left bothered me not. Never once did I think about how those that love me would be without me if I pulled the trigger and blew my brains out on the very spot I stood with the man, I assumed loved me. Never once did I anticipate my son waking up to get out of my car to come in the church to see me kill myself.

I dropped the thirty-eight and fell on my face. Being a part of me, my son came over and hugged me. I wept sorrowfully. He lay beside me and tried to put his head under my arms, but he couldn't. He pulled on me a little and I did not move, I just cried all the more. Josiah said, "Don't cry, mommy. I love you."

"I love you, too, Josiah, with all my heart and never let anyone make you feel any less than what you are."

He doesn't understand those words, but I had to tell him because hearing him say he loves me made me bellow out all the more. I could not explain my actions to him nor God. I was taking the very life God gave me. How foolish

71

the enemy almost had me doing what he could not do on his own. It was a rash decision on my part to believe that suicide would cure me of the pain I was feeling.

I came back here to the place where my life was ruined. I told the Lord if He didn't stop me, I was going to do what I came here to do, but He did interfere. This day, I was going to end my life here, but the higher power of Jesus came into play.

I finally got up and my son sat on my lap and went back to sleep. I curled beside him and held him. I realized I hadn't lived and for that cause I knew that a better me must emerge as a great symbolic bird the Phoenix, who rises from the ashes of nothing to be something greater.

The longer I laid there with him the more I knew I had to live and go on. I have to get over Ahmad and do it fast because he and his woman friend were taking a toll on my life. I already devoted the past few days of my life to them and what they were doing or have done. I no longer needed them to take away any more of my time and life.

I closed my eyes again and this time, I knew I must beat this and rise like never before. I believe that I will come out on top and with the new plans, I will. I vowed not to cry or have feelings. If Ahmad thinks he is ready, he won't be especially when he finds out that I'm all out of "Who gives a fuck."

The next day, I woke up and my son was in his grandfather's arms. I was puzzled at first then he said,

72

"Good morning, Tygeria."

Yarning and stretching, I asked sleepily "What time is it?"

"It's time for you to wake up and shake yourself from the dust."

I jolted up because that was the last thing I remembered thinking. I smiled and said, "The Lord works in mysterious ways, and this is one of them."

"It's good to see you smiling again."

"It feels good to smile again, Pastor."

"Mommy, you woke."

Smiling at my new world, I said "Mommy woke."

"You both need breakfast this morning."

"Josiah is hungry because he eats like a horse to be as young as he is."

"Can I take him for the week?"

"Sure, what you have planned?"

"I want to take him to visit my family in Corpus Christi, Texas. I know my sons aren't going so I want to take my only grandson to see his other family members. I will take great care of him."

"Pastor, I know you will. Do I need to pack him

some clothes?"

"No, he has plenty at the house already."

"Okay. When are you leaving?"

"This afternoon."

"Why so soon?"

"I was going to ask while you were on your honeymoon but waited. Honestly, I felt the need to ask you now."

"Let me take him by Josh and Jessica so they can tell me bye. You can pick him up from there."

"Okay."

We all got up. Pastor locked the doors of the church as I walked to the car. After I locked Josh down, he said "Here, no one needs to know about this."

He handed me the gun. I locked it in the glove compartment as he continued, "All last night I prayed for you and your situation. I even talked to my son, but he is stubborn as you well know that. There was a reason, you didn't do what you planned to do, and I am thankful that you didn't. If my son does not want his family, God will give you all to another, simple as that. Let God do it, not Tygeria. There is a reason he canceled the devil's plans on your life. Now more than ever you need to fast and pray. Above all don't forget to read his word; for it alone can minister to you better than anyone can."

74

For the first time in days, I did not cry and nor did I feel like crying. That pity party I was at has been canceled, and the good-hearted girl that lived at this address became missing. Making up my mind, I decided to move out of Ackerman and regroup my life. I have to do the best for me and my son. Soon as Ahmad realizes that my "I give a care bucket has a hole in it," and it won't be patched up any time soon, he will see just how green his pasture was with me.

I was lost while Josiah was away, but while he was away, I decided that a change of scenery would be good for both of us. Ahmad knew I was leaving, and he did not try to see his son before we were to leave. It angered me some, but I wasn't surprised. He let a woman come between him and his son which was something he had vowed not to do, but his words meant nothing to me.

The day Josiah came back with his grandpa, we left. I was getting out of Ackerman and leaving everything behind me. I planned not to return until I changed and that is what I intend to do.

CHAPTER 4

Present Time

A loud voice over the intercom broke me from recalling my past as I heard the captain announce they we were landing in ten minutes. I became nervous. J Lamb is to meet us at the airport waiting area, and I hoped he would not notice me. He may not fully understand that a bitch was born out of the ashes and debris of a rumbled life. For years I endured, fat jokes and being teased about being overweight.

Of course, that changed when I met J Lamb and Ahmad, and so did a lot of things in my life. I refuse to dwell on the past. Personally, there will be no more having someone wiping their feet on me. No more doing all I could for people that took me for granted and no more being downplayed or seen as a joke. That life is now behind me as I am more focused on the task at hand.

Soon as we made it through the terminal, I got our small bags. My cell rang and it was J Lamb. "Hello, if it isn't the second most sought-after bitch in all the land?"

"Why are you settling for second best when you and I both know that I am number one?"

"Whatever!" I exclaimed with joy and anticipation.

"I heard them announce your plane arrival, where you at?"

"I'm standing at the airport looking at you."

J Lamb began looking all around for me as he hung up. He looked right at me and still did not see me. I was glad for that means I have achieved my first step. J Lamb turned back around and called me again. I picked up and said, "Hello."

"Why are you lying? I looked all around, and I did not see you."

"Turn slowly and look again."

This time when he turned around, Josiah came from behind me. He spotted Josiah then he looked up at me. Soon as our eyes locked, he spoke with amazement, "Tygeria?"

Making my smile familiar to him, I spoke "Jamal?"

My best friend in the world took off running towards us. I was just as happy to see him as he was to see me. He gave me a swift hug then picked up Josiah. Soon as he put Josiah down, he marched around me like prey being stalked. He came back to face me to say, "Tell me your secret."

"I can't, you might want a copy."

He continued to smile at me with all those teeth of his. He said, "Ty, you look damn good."

"I do look good, don't I?"

77

"Good is not the word. You the bomb."

"That sounds like I have to blow up."

As he continued to grin and gawk at me in admiration, he spoke, "I kid you not. Now you are a for-real Tiger Ho."

"That's nothing wait until a man sees my stripes."

"What gives the new look?"

"After what I went through, why not a new me?"

"Ahmad is going to pout for sure for his wife."

I gave him a stare that meant death. He stopped and asked, "What I say wrong?"

"We don't use the A-word."

"Ty, I was just saying."

"Don't say. That is just a name in the wind to me."

Disturbing our conversation was Josiah as he asked, "Mommy, that daddy?"

We both looked down at him. I kneeled to his level to say, "No, that's Uncle Jamal."

"Uncle Mal?" J Lamb said.

"Yes, Uncle Mal."

J Lamb kneeled beside me to ask, "Little man, you don't remember me?"

Josiah kind of leaned into me some as I said, "J Lamb he is just a little over three now.

J Lamb stood up and so did I. He grabbed our bags said, "Come on, your brother told me I better bring you by his house first to see your niece Jos'etta Tyshell."

"Let's not keep them waiting."

We got in the car and Josiah was excited. I could tell from the way he was looking out the window at this strange environment. J Lamb spoke, "You know she had a little boy."

"Yeah, I know."

"She was all on Facebook talking about her happy family," J Lamb spoke.

"Good for her."

"She named him Brian Arivon Charleston."

"What? She didn't name him after Ahmad?"

"His name isn't even on the birth certificate."

"Why is that, since he is his and all?"

"He has his doubts, but his excuse is he couldn't get off from work in time to sign the paper."

We both said, "He lying."

J Lamb and I laughed at that. Open my phone up and

click on my photos. I did as he asked then said, "There isn't but one photo in here."

"I know. I did that so you will see what we all see."

Soon as I clicked on the photo, I saw it. It was a collage of Josiah and the other baby. The difference was that of night and day. My son is tall to be just three. Not only that he has Ahmad's facial complexion and everything; on the other hand, the other little boy is extremely dark, short, and looks nothing like Ahmad but similar to his bright-skinned mother.

"How about, she told him that their little boy looks like people in her family."

"He might. You know that is possible."

"Yeah, but the two of those boys should have some type of feature in common which they don't. I don't mean to boast but you should have seen my brother's face when he saw that little one."

I grin a little, as I continued to hear him say, "He nearly flipped out. And the sad part is he has been trying to play it cool. But you know him as I know him."

"You mean like I thought I knew him."

Rolling his eyes in his usual way, he spoke, "Some of his friends told him he needs to get him tested, and I do believe he is going to do it soon."

"That's him. I have other things going on in my

life."

"You are still married to him and technically the chap is your stepchild."

"A lie! Like on my wedding day and like Bianca said, it's just on paper."

Changing the subject, J Lamb added "He been asking have I talked to you."

"He can ask all he wants, and I don't see what for. My number has not changed, and he has it. If he wants to talk to me, he knows he could have."

"You know he has pride."

I spoke, "Pride and a baby that doesn't look like him."

We rode a few more minutes before J Lamb said, "Ty, you do look good, and I can't believe the transformation."

"It's me."

"It's half of you. The other half disappeared."

"The other person has gone on and this is what was left behind."

"You mean a bitch?"

"I guess so."

"You gonna go see daddy?"

"I am. I will probably wait to bring Josiah to see him."

"You know he wants to know when you get in town."

"I know but right now, I have to get settled then I will let him know I am in town."

"You going to his church?"

"I am still going to go to the church."

"That's a big step. You sure you ready for that?"

"I don't know but I have to. He has gone on with his life, why shouldn't I?"

"Because you both are married, and my brother has changed since you been gone."

"How is that, when he never called to check on his son?"

"He would ask me how you both were doing, and I would tell him."

"You should have told him to ask me, himself."

"He won't do that. I do believe he is still hurt and misses you."

"He can miss all he wants. The pain is too real, and I am just now to the point where I can mention his name without tearing up."

82

"I know you loved him, but he wants to do the right thing."

"He can do whatever he thinks the right thing is for him; as for me, I have a son to think about."

At this time, we arrived at my brother's house. It was different being back in Ackerman. Nothing had changed and before I could get Josiah out, my brother literally ran out the door. Mind you he hasn't seen me since that day before I left. I did not tell him I was leaving because he would have talked me out of it, and I didn't need that.

When he set eyes on me, he stopped short. I spoke, "You don't recognize your sister?"

"Ty, it is you?"

"Yes, it's me, your only sibling."

"Ty, it is you!" He screamed as he picked up the speed. Once he reached me, Josh picked me up and twirled me around; just like he used to when we were younger. He put me down and squeezed me.

"Where is Josiah?"

"Here he goes."

My brother released me and started unhooking his nephew. Josiah had a blank look on his face as he said, "Uncle Josh."

My mind captured a moment that I would not

exchange for the world. My brother saw his nephew and was emotional by means he doesn't do often. Josh gave him a heartfelt hug. He placed him down and said, "I am so glad you are home."

We began to walk into his house as I said, "Actually, I am only visiting today."

"What you mean visiting?"

"I am going to move to Louisville."

His look was indescribable. J Lamb took Josiah inside as he and I stood outside. The house front door closed and I spoke, "What?"

"Are you up to something?"

"No. I had this thought out before I came back to Mississippi."

"Where bout are you going to stay?"

"In a community by Wal-Mart."

"You aren't going to stay in the same community that he lives in are you with that girl?"

"Yes, I am."

"Ty, that is trouble."

"Why should I worry about trouble? She is sleeping with my husband."

"I don't think you should do it."

"Brother I am grateful for your concern, but I must live my life, and this is the way I want to do it."

"Fine, I know how you are, and I can't change your mind. Let's go in so you can see your niece Jos."

"That is her nickname already?"

"Yup."

We laughed as he opened the door for me. When we got in, Jessica was already sitting in the sitting area with the baby. My niece is beautiful even at almost five months. I looked at Jos and said, "She looks like mom."

"Same thing I said when I laid eyes on her."

I went over to Jessica and hug her before I took my niece away. Josiah saw me holding her and began to cry. Josh took him to the kitchen, and he became quiet. It's funny how this is supposed to be me. Happily married and holding my newborn, but that is water under the bridge. J Lamb came out of the bathroom and said, "I hope y'all have another bathroom because that one is a wreck."

Laughing I spoke, "You blew up their bathroom?"

"Yeah, you thought I was going to hold it in?"

Jessica laughed too as we spent another hour talking to her and my brother. They all could not get over the new look that I have. My hair was longer and thicker. My breast was still big, but my stomach was smaller due to the surgery, and I felt great. If I had known that my weight was an issue, I would have done something about it a long time ago, but I was taught to love myself.

I was also taught that if people love you, they are to love you for you. I also thought my husband did, but I was mistaken. Sighing, Jessica was laughing at me.

"What?"

She pointed at J Lamb. I smiled and asked, "What?"

"We all know you only got this new look to impress the A word."

"That is why you all were laughing at me?"

"Ty I was not laughing. I love you for who you are. I just know that a new you mean a new attitude and I hope it is not a bad one."

"You too late" J Lamb spoke as he shook his head.

"That is not true!" I spoke with laughter, in my defense.

"I tell y'all what. If you don't believe me, wait and see for yourself. Tiger Ho didn't stay out of our sight for nothing."

"J Lamb you are to quit."

"I'm just saying. You didn't tell us where you were,

what you been doing and we couldn't come to see you. Sounds suspect to me. What y'all think Josh and Jessica?"

"I think it's time for us to go," I said to my best friend.

"Where are you going, you just got here?"

"I do have a place to stay."

"Where, when you can stay with us?"

"I know but I have things to do and in a way I am different."

J Lamb was pretending to sneeze as he said, "Slut."

I could only laugh at him, but my brother wasn't laughing. He wanted me to stay with them, but I couldn't. I am grown and I have become independent. I said, "Josh, I have been living on my own for over a year now and longer if you count when I was with Ahmad."

"I know but you just got in and we want you here with us."

"I'll be coming by and I'm sure Josiah won't let me stay away too long from you. Besides, I love seeing Jos."

"Where are you going to be living at, while you in Louisville?"

"I have a place in a community by Wal-Mart?"

"Is that near Ahmad and that girl?"

"Same block, same housing complex and across the parking lot, if you want the truth."

J Lamb said as he walked out the door, "A lie would have sounded better."

"Ty, why are you doing this? Why place you and your son in a predicament to be shamed or have that woman cause trouble for you."

"She has my husband not the other way around. Josh as long as they don't bother me, we good. It has been a year since they have seen me so why would it bother them now?"

"Seeing the new you, is not going to be a problem?"

"Why should it? When he had me, he broke me and damaged me. Now I am a better me."

"I don't think it is a good idea."

"I didn't at first but the more I thought about it the more it made sense to me."

"How does living across the parking lot from your husband and his new family make sense to you?"

"In this manner, I am not running from them. I have my own life and will be applying for a divorce."

"Okay. Just be careful and if you need me, call me."

"Don't I always?"

"You do but can Josiah stay until you get settled or see his dad first?"

I thought I can do a lot with him not there. Trying to act like I didn't want him to, I spoke "I don't know. You already have your baby here."

"Josiah was our baby first" Jessica added.

"Okay, he can stay. Let me say goodbye first."

I went into the family room and Josiah was almost asleep. I said, "Josiah, mommy going to let you stay with Uncle Josh, okay?"

"You come to get me?"

"Yes, mommy will come back to get you."

"Okay."

My son reached up and hugged me as I kissed him goodnight. It is fairly early, but he is exhausted from the trip then playing with my brother. I began to walk out and stopped in front of a mirror. Sometimes when I looked in the mirror, I amazed myself. I could not believe my appearance. Just to think, it took a bitch to bring the real bitch out of me, and in a way I am grateful.

"You coming? Or you still going to gawk at the bitch in the mirror?"

It was J Lamb. I turned to him and said, "Oh, I'm coming to believe that."

I hugged Jessica as Josh took Josiah's bag out of the car before I left with J Lamb. We waved bye and backed out the driveway. J Lamb asked, "If you need to pay me to take you places let me know in advance because my fee is a hefty one."

"No need my ride is at the apartment."

"Damn you fast and good."

"I have to be."

"You ready to shock my brother?"

"It's not about him."

"You lying to me."

"I am not. It has something to do with him but not all about him."

"What does it have to do with then?"

"It's all about me."

"You sound like you a teacher in a classroom full of three-year-olds."

We laughed as he entered Winston County. Nervous feelings showed me as we drove closer and closer to the four-way stop by McDonald's. Minutes later we arrived at my new place. Butterflies began to wiggle inside my stomach as I inhaled noisily and exhaled just as loud.

"You might as well, get rid of those nerves because you should have known what you were doing."

"I do know what I am doing, and I have strategically planned this out and I intend to carry it out."

"You good, he still at work."

"Good, I'm going to need the child support to help take care of Josiah."

We got out of the car. I showed J Lamb my ride and he liked it. At that moment, I spotted Blackie. He was staring at me, and I gave him the look back. J Lamb saw it and said, "Oooh you dirty bitch. I know what you trying to do."

Under my breath, I spoke with a tease, "Go in the house my son, grown people at work" then I threw him the keys. This tall dark-skinned man with wavy hair approached me. I pretended not to take in the sight of his killer brown eyes his, but he was cute to be as dark as he is.

He walked even closer. He opened his mouth and all I saw were beautiful white teeth. Getting in front of me, he placed his foot on the curb of the sidewalk to say, "Do I know you?"

"Do you want to know me, is the question?"

He gave me that player laugh along with the all-white smile to match. I then said, "You over here all in my face; someone could come out and hurt me because of you."

"Lovely, everything on my end is sewed up, and I don't have room for drama. What's good on your end?"

"It's good, but I don't even know your name."

"It's Blackie."

Making my eyes search him all over I repeated, "Blackie?" as my eyes reached his.

"Yeah, Blackie is all you need to know for now."

"I may not want to know anything else after now."

He laughed as he said, "Strong, I like that. So, what's your name?"

"Tygeria, but my close friends call me Tiger."

"Tiger?" He said as his eyes lit up when I spoke with a hint of an erotic tease.

I repeated it with a smile, "Tiger."

"May I have your number, Tiger?"

"What you going to do if I give it to you?"

"Give it to me and see."

My breast was balanced perfectly on my chest as my skin glistened from the scented perfume. I saw the way he kept watching them rise and fall. I couldn't resist the temptation to make him linger after them as I walked closer to him. Even though I don't have my weight, I still have the breast, and these girls are going to help me out in a lot of ways.

Reaching up slowly, I made my index finger draw a wiggly line down his chest and stopped shy of his crotch. He smiled with likeness of the small play I did. Stepping back up onto the sidewalk I spoke, "I hate to give my number to a man that runs games- that I don't have time or strength to play."

Blackie gave my body an overview as he said, "I don't play games; I'm too old for that."

"I don't know what you are too old for, but I know you are never too old to learn a new trick.

"A new trick?"

"Neither do I that's why I chose what I do carefully. If you want to know anything about me, ask me. I don't have to lie because I am a full-figured grown-ass woman."

He licked his lips seductively and it was a turn-on. I saw the way he kept watching my breast with his eyes. He said, "I like you and I don't like women I just meet too quickly and too often. It's something about you that makes me want you."

"You have to know what it is, to know if you want it."

I began to walk off from him. He spoke, "Tiger, I'll be seeing you around."

"Maybe?" I said as I made it halfway to my apartment door. He yelled out, "Can't wait to see your stripes."

He and I both laughed as I went inside the apartment and without giving him my number. If he wants it, he'll be back. When I locked the door behind me, J Lamb asked, "How the hell you get a house full of furniture, and you haven't been back in Mississippi?"

"Ya girl got game she didn't know she had."

"I see she does."

We sat on the couch as he asked, "First of all, what is the deal with Blackie?"

"There is no deal."

"Quit lying! Since you been gone, you have done become a liar."

I giggled when I said, "I am not a liar. You may not be able to comprehend what I say."

"Try me."

"You want something to drink or eat?"

"Hell, no, don't change the subject. I know how to get the food or juice so get on with the story."

"There is no story. I didn't plan on meeting him or even talking to him. In good conscience, I forgot all about him until now."

"He does have a woman wife or whatever her role is."

"I figured that much."

"She not from here, tho."

"How about children?"

"If he does, they aren't from here."

"Where does he work?"

"He was working at Taylor's, but he left and now runs the new Bar and Grill, right outside of town."

"We might have to check that out."

"We just might, it's open only on Friday's and Saturday's and it's not your average place. There is security and a second floor VIP, which I want to get in to see. They play old school and it's a nice place."

"You been in there before?"

"I been there but not in the VIP."

"We got to get you in the VIP, don't we?"

"Hell yeah, you do. Use his ass because it makes no sense to make him keep that money all to himself."

"I don't need his money."

"What do you need? When you left, I needed a damn umbrella because your eyes stayed full of water."

"Don't remind me."

"I'm just telling the truth. All of a sudden you come back, and you are not a regular bitch but a top-notch bitch at that."

"That's the only way to be because I learned while I was away that people get too heavy to carry so you drop their ass like a bad habit and get your habit. Mines just happened to be a bitch."

"One I like, might I add."

"Now what was I saying?"

"You are about to tell me your story."

CHAPTER 5

I took off my shoes and long sleeve shirt. I crossed my legs and said, "When your brother, my husband broke my heart I needed to get away and do some soul searching. I ran off to Utah.

"Utah? Isn't that Indian Territory? Why there? You got Apache Indian in your veins now?"

"You have gone let me talk or you going to talk for me?"

He lifted his hands as to shush himself. I said, "I choose this place because I did not want to be found. I knew no one would ever think of me in an area like this."

"You ain't ever lied."

Chuckling I continued, "I had to get my heart and life together. I still prayed and read the Word daily, but I am the first to admit that I didn't go to church."

"You didn't go to church! Daddy gone flip out cause you and I both know that he took you under his wing especially when you and Ahmad got together, he was more thrilled than you were," J Lamb yelled.

"I didn't go to church but that does not mean I don't have the love of God in my heart."

"I didn't say you can't have church in you because we are the temple of God, and the church is just a building that believers gather to worship in."

"True so that means, your daddy going to be alright."

"Awe, I know you going to Hell now. You don't ever miss church and talk about your lovely Pastor in the same breath; never."

"I still pray. Maybe not as much but I do still love the Lord and with so much that has happened in my life, I thank HIM every morning."

"So, that don't mean you nothing if your life doesn't line up with HIS Word. You can't go to heaven by being half right. You either going to get right or be left."

Sniggering, I responded, "You so worldly but your talk is so Godly. Can I finish please?"

He put up his hands again as to quiet himself so I can talk.

"I didn't go to church because I felt like a let-down to myself. I was hurt and became bitter. I didn't want to be that way, so disappearing was my option. I've been the good girl all my life and still got screwed in the process. Mainly, I came to the conclusion that if he wanted her and her son, then I was going to step back and let them have each other. I just wished he had told me so she wouldn't have wrecked my wedding day. As for church I'm going to go one day."

"But still we are not to forsake the assembly" J Lamb added.

"I know."

J Lamb spoke as he pointed his head towards me, "Well, know to do and not to do is what?"

I finished by saying, "A sin unto you."

"You already know so I can't say anything else on that matter. Case closed."

"Still, Ahmad."

J Lamb butted in again by saying, "Oh yeah, Ahmad and I talked, and he is sorry for what he did. I think that is why he has changed. When you talk to him" I cut him off and said with a hint of anger, "I don't want to talk to him just yet."

"You think, he gonna let you stay across the parking lot and not be involved in who comes over to see you and his son?"

"He needs to worry about what goes on in apartment two and not in apartment seven."

"Girl, it's ok to dream" J Lamb stated.

We laughed as he asked, "Are you mentally ready to see him and are you really ready for what lies ahead?"

"I am not so sure, but I know it must be done."

"Now what about Blackie?"

"Oh, that?"

"Yes, that."

"We just met."

"I may be wrong about a lot of things but my brother will fall the fuck out if he knew Blackie was feeling you and you were giving it to him."

"Maybe?"

"Maybe my ass, I don't want to come over here just to pull him off you."

We laughed at that thought as I said, "He better get with the program, then."

"Yeah, the program of a stalker."

We laughed at the line. I spoke, "That's all he better do because he doesn't pay bills here and he doesn't care about shit on this end."

"You cursing now? I know this is about to be good. Don't you want a roommate?"

"No, I don't need a roommate. I can't do what I do with a roommate."

"You have a son, and he doesn't need to see men in and out your place."

"He won't see me like that. I don't do my business like that; I still have standards."

"Just checking, now what about this apartment and the stuff in it?"

"I came down and put in an app. Her dad is a fresh, old, dirty man."

He cut me off and asked with surprise, "Don't tell me you screwed him?"

"No, I didn't screw him. I was being me, and I didn't use any type of game to get him to let me get the apartment."

"Especially now, since his son is sweating you, and his daughter is sweating your husband."

With a caring laugh I said, "I am so glad you haven't changed."

"Why would I, when what you see is what you get. You either get it or you don't."

"Did he have something to do with the furniture?"

"No, I went to Baber's and paid cash with the exception they delivered it the same day."

"You came in town and didn't let me know?"

"I didn't let anyone know."

"What about work?"

101

"I start at Taylor's in the Personnel department as the new Human Resource Manager Assistant."

"When you left you had your heart in your hand and clothes on your back. Now you are telling me you going to be working where your husband works?"

"Yes."

"You gave up the Day Care job for an office job?"

"Yes, back here when you were calling out my list of degrees, an associate in office technology was one of them. Plus, this office job that pays, seventeen dollars an hour."

"Shit, get me on."

"Can't."

"How you get on?"

"Let's just say, there was a private interest."

"You fucked your way through the door, didn't you?"

I only laughed as he said, "Look who's calling me?"

It was Ahmad. My heart began to beat in my ears. I became nervous because I haven't seen him or heard his voice since the day I left the hospital. This seems harder than I imagined because I am here and his voice is just seconds away.

"Want me to answer it?"

"Do you, I'm good."

J Lamb picked up the phone and put it on speaker before saying, "Hello."

"Is Ty back in town?"

"You could at least ask your brother how he doing, since you called his phone and all?"

"How you doing? Is Ty back?"

"Yeah, she back and why you want to know?"

He was silent as my ears made my brain meditate on the sound of his mesmerizing voice. That sound alone made chills cover me. He still has that effect on me. I thought it would have gone away but it hasn't. I wasn't prepared for this unexpected loop.

"I said why?" J Lamb asked his brother.

"I want to see her and Josiah."

"What if she doesn't want to see you?"

"She my wife and I am our son's father."

"What does that mean? Men take care of other men's children every day. You do it so use another excuse."

Ahmad did not say anything.

103

"Since you my brother I will give you the heads up and what I found out."

I started shaking my head no because I knew what he was about to tell him. Knowing J Lamb and the drama he still loves to create in my life he said, "Blackie was talking to your wife today and I think she is feeling him."

"Who?"

"You know your girlfriend's brother, Blackie."

"She ain't my girlfriend."

"Well, whatever her title is to you, her brother Blackie."

"What the hell he doing talking to my wife?"

"I don't know, but your wife is grown and looks damn good, I might add. Too bad she not my type."

Ahmad spoke as if he was trying to give instruction, "He doesn't need to be talking to her."

"In fact, Tygeria has moved in the vacant apartment across from where you live now."

"Quit lying."

I tried taking the phone from J Lamb, but he began running, and he finally locked himself in the bathroom. The house was quiet, so I still heard them talking. Ahmad said, "Ty has moved across from me?"

"Yeah? You don't want to see her or something?"

"I always love seeing her."

"I won't tell you this, but you don't know what she looks like. You hurt her so bad, she became a man."

"WHAT! A fucking man!" Ahmad screamed.

I fell on the floor laughing as J Lamb said, "I'm just playing. I always wanted to do that to someone and figured why not you."

"J Lamb, don't be playing with me like that."

"What you care for if she becomes a man, you have a woman?"

"Let's not get into that."

"What you want; you wasting my minutes anyway?"

"Tell her I want to see her and our son?"

"You tell her because you know I am over here so call her phone."

"I don't know the number?"

"You know she ain't changed numbers; you changed numbers."

"Wait, you said you at her place now?"

Trying to be silly, J Lamb asked "Is you at her place now? Where you at anyway, asking all these questions?"

"J Lamb, you always protected her, and I am your brother."

"I am for what is right, and I did right by telling you that your brother-in-law is hollering at her."

With an attitude, he said "He ain't my brother-in-law. Josh Homely is the only brother-in-law I have."

"You are with his sister so one can only assume that Blackie is your law."

"I just got off from work and I'll come over, while you there."

"You can't just show up at her place. You not her man."

"Right, I am her husband, and I am coming over."

"In what world?"

"Tell her I'm coming to see her, now."

J Lamb opened the door and playfully began hitting him with a pillow. He laughed as we went back to the couch.

"Why you tell him that for? He doesn't need to know who is hollering at me."

"I know y'all still love each other but circumstances

have come between y'all. I told him all that to get him to thinking and when he sees you, he is going to flip out."

"Let me go change."

Going as fast as I could, I went in my bathroom and showered quicker than I normally do. Soon as I dried off, I lathered my body with sweet smelling lotion, his favorite of course. Tonight, I will let my hair hang, and I will wear something very tempting. With my robe on, J Lamb knocked on the door.

"Come in."

"I know you trying to look all sexual, and all so you need a man's opinion."

"What are you suggesting?"

"Something that screams, I want sex but not by you for sure."

Laughter came out my mouth as I stared at my best friend in the entire world. Seconds later, he asked "How about this?"

It was a one-piece body suit. It was a dark brown, with low cuts in the front for cleavage and the back out for temptation, by that I lifted my hair to show off my big breast. The suit is one of my favorites as I smiled to agree. J Lamb left out for me to get dressed. When I came back in the living room, he said "You not a Tiger Ho tonight, you a dog hunter."

That was funny to hear as he said, "I'm going to let him think that I didn't tell you what he said."

"It doesn't matter."

"You right because he'll know that I told you; still, he doesn't know the new you."

Putting on my gold hoop earrings and a thick necklace to match, I do look good.

"Let's go outside so when we see him pull up, it'll look like I am trying to leave before he got here."

He peeked outside and said, "Blackie outside."

"Let me see," I said as I peep through the blinds.

There on the new all-black Camaro was Blackie. J Lamb turned to me and stated, "This going to be fun."

Four minutes later, Ahmad pulled in the parking lot. Just seeing that man made me shake within; for he is still my husband, and I still love him, but I have to go on.

"You ready?"

"Yeah."

Ahmad did not make it out the car. Blackie saw me come out and began making purring sounds. I waved at him and continued like I was walking J Lamb to his car. My best friend said, "I know you not sending me home for real, Stella getting her groove back?"

"Depends on who comes over, Juwanna Man."

"Trick got jokes, huh."

Ahmad was coming over as his girlfriend stood in the door and watched. J Lamb did not get in the car. His brother got closer to me and stared at me. It was like he did not know who I was at first but when he leaned closer; he saw me and scaled my body. I saw that he was breathing a slight harder as he saw me dressed in this outfit. I also know that he has never seen me looking like this.

"Ty, that's really you dressed like that?"

"Ahmad is that really you, staring at me like that?"

"Boy don't just stand there looking stupid, say something to your wife" J Lamb added as Ahmad continued to ponder over my new look.

"Ahmad, tell your wife how she looks."

"Ty, you look, look wonderful."

"Thanks, you never how what a heart break and many sleepless nights can do to a soul until you been there."

"Boy, open your mouth, say something better than that?" J Lamb said to his brother, but Ahmad did not respond. He kept his eyes fixed on me. I saw Blackie looking and I yelled out, "You ready?"

Ahmad looked back at Blackie as he yelled back, "If

you ready, I am always ready."

In haste, my husband asked, "Where is Josiah and where do you think you are going dressed like that?"

"Josiah is none of your concern, and I am a grown ass woman."

Blackie crank the car up. Ahmad said, "You don't need to be with him?"

"I don't need to do a lot of things with him."

J Lamb said as he began to get in his car, "Keep on making statements, and you don't like the answers."

Before Ahmad could get irritated, Bianca called out for him to come. Blackie got out the car and opened the door for me. I looked back at Ahmad and winked before sitting in the car and allowing him to drive off.

"You look good. You smell better. Do you taste as well as you look and smell?"

"That is something only my man will know."

Before we pulled onto the busy highway, he asked me a question that I knew was on his mind, "How you know Ahmad?"

"I'm his wife."

Puzzled in speech, Blackie said "You Tygeria?"

"Yes, you know me?"

A huge smile covered his face and all I saw were those white teeth as he said, "We met weigh over a year ago at y'alls apartment in Ackerman. You cooked some chicken on a stick and I told you I liked it. That was the last time Ahmad had us near each other."

Acting like I was remembering what I already knew I spoke with a huge but sexual smile, "Sure did. Small world isn't it."

"I have always liked you. I mean there was something about you that I liked."

"You did?"

"Yeah, Ahmad knew it because I told him that he has a great woman and if I were him I would keep her."

"Oh."

"I think that is why he kept you and me from each other."

I became silent as he said, "Your personality is another thing I liked. From the time I met you, you made me feel at home. I was myself around you for that short time and didn't have to fake about what I have. You were the type of woman that a man brings home to his mother."

"So, what type of woman, you see me as now?"

"Honestly, I don't know how you are now, but I know the sweet down-to-earth girl in you exists. I like the strong woman you are now. Nowadays, you can't find that in one girl, and you have the whole package."

"You think?"

He smiled those flashy white teeth at me and said, "I know."

I laid back and he asked, "Where you want to go, Tygeria?"

"We can just go to Wal-Mart and sit in the car."

"We can do that but if you hungry I'll buy you something to eat?"

"Thank you but no, I'm good."

Blackie pulled in the parking lot towards the bottom.

"You really do have a nice car."

"Thanks."

He parked and said, "You make it hard for a nigga to keep his mind off sex."

"Don't mean to be a distraction."

"It's ok. Give me something to look forward to."

We were quiet for a few as people walked by the car. He asked, "What's the deal between you and Ahmad anyway?"

"There is no deal with him and if I were you, I

wouldn't worry about him."

"I'm not."

It was quiet for a few seconds before I spoke, "You have some type of woman somewhere and I'm not trying to be her, so let's just keep it real."

"Alright, I don't want to talk about him anyway, but I am sure he is wondering what we doing."

"Let him wonder, which ways my legs are going."

Blackie laughed as he moved his head left to right.

"You going to give me your number?"

"Give me your phone."

With no hesitation, he handed me his cell. I typed my number in it and for my name I put in, Tiger Stripes. I gave it back to him and called it. When he saw my name, he flashed those teeth again.

"Tiger Stripes?"

"You never know if you see them or not."

"I like that."

He and I sat there and talked about what we want to do in the future. He even told me about his little friend girl that doesn't want anything more in life but to work as a manager at McDonald's in Starkville. I was pleased at the company he was giving me. He didn't come after me or anything. Blackie was a real gentleman.

We laughed and talked about what we liked and didn't like. I was really shocked to have a lot in common with him. Meeting him and being here with him was not a part of my plan but a nice touch. He and I sat there for four hours, and midnight was fast approaching, and I have to work in the morning. Sounding tired for I was as I said, "I hate to break this up but I'm tired and ready to go back. It's been a long day for me, and I have to work."

The truth is, I have orientation and at Taylor's off-site for two weeks; therefore, Ahmad wouldn't see. That would be okay because when he does it would be worth this wait. Seconds later, Blackie pulled out and we headed back to the apartment. I thought he would have turned in front of his apartment house, but he didn't. He got out and opened the door for me.

Since he and I been chatting it up, he always opens the door for me; something Ahmad has never done. I gave him a sincere smile as he walked me to the door. I saw Ahmad and used the opportunity to give Blackie a hug. Liking the feel of his body against mine, I couldn't help but to hold on a little longer. Blackie stepped back and said, "I really had a great time talking to you. Tygeria, you are easy to talk to. Not to sound like rain on a fire, but Ahmad was stupid for not being with you but his lost is another man's gain, preferably mine."

"You never know what the future holds."

Giving him one bigger hug, Ahmad closed the blind, and I released the interaction.

"Go on. A gentleman doesn't leave until the young lady goes in the house. Have to make sure you are safe."

"Make sure I am safe, or you want me to invite you in?"

"Right now, just to make sure you are safe, but later I will take you up on the invite. Go on, I need to see you walk in the house."

"I like that, a gentleman."

"Just for you, Tiger."

Closing the door, I locked it and smiled. I had a great time with him, and I really look forward to seeing him again. This is the first real time; I actually felt like smiling. Maybe moving to Louisville was a great idea, but I know I have to watch my back because a great guy like that means lurking bitches.

CHAPTER 6

After being in orientation for two weeks, Saturday came, and I was in need of something to do. Josiah was still with my brother, so I took advantage of the break. Getting in touch with J Lamb, he and a few guys he knew took me out. The very place he took me was to Blackie's Bar and Grill.

The place extremely nice and so far, well organized. When you walk in you walk through metal detective frame and then you are hand scanned. The security guy's name was Devin, and he looked familiar. He took his scanner and went over my body slowly.

He's cute and I liked the attention he was giving me. J Lamb said, "Hurry up Devin with your slow ass. If you knew who she was, you would keep that scanner to your damn self."

"She can tell me if she wants to, but you need to wait your turn, J Lamb."

J Lamb turned his head and said in a low tone to his round, "Like she wants his slow ass."

I laughed at that. After J Lamb and the guys were scanned we walked in. The song Wipe Me Down blared through the speakers. The guys put me in a circle. They all began dancing around me. To cause more attention, I started dancing like I know I am the best in the place. Each one of the guys took turns to dance with me in the circle and that alone made the bystanders look.

We weren't all on each other, but we were making a scene. Out the corner of my eye, I thought I saw Ahmad. Quickly dismissed it because all eyes are on me, and I am here to make noise. As the people cleared the floor for us, we had to make the looks count. That is the reason you come to the club late, to make an entrance and to run off the ones that think they are the shit.

Therefore, you must be on point and have crew with you that is down with you. Confidently, I placed my hand on my hips; me in my orange spaghetti string dress, with the back out, with shoestring ties at the breast area and no bra on. My shoes were medium heels and an orange handbag to match the orange rose in my hair. Everyone was checking me out, mainly, because I am new and have never been in the place before.

The song ended and we made our way to the bar for drinks. Real bitches must be seen and known in the place. Some guy bought us a round of drinks, and I left. This night, I was the only one wearing something as loud as orange and had all the eyes on us. J Lamb screamed, "You better blow up tonight if you don't ever make a spark."

Before this new me emerged, I was a home body and only went to church, family gatherings, and other than work, a little shopping. Now a positive medium-figured woman is in the place. Some would call me uppity, but I am high maintenance; there is a difference. Going behind J Lamb, he picked a booth in the front because a woman like me likes to be the center of attention.

As I looked around smeared looks were on faces of wanna be stunners, so I smile because it is not my fault if low hoes can't come up to my level. Just by what I have seen from the women here, they need to upgrade to a newer height. The music began to play, and I was in the mood from the old jams they were playing. J Lamb was dancing with some girl. She was all on him and to me it was funny.

My suspicious were confirmed. I did see my husband. He came by my table and intentionally knocked on my table. That was his sign to let me know that he is in the building. Giving him my I-don't-give-a-fuck look, I sat back in a relax state with my arms spread out. He came back from the bar, and I encouraged my breast to give him the attention he used to get by moving them up and down slowly.

When I opened my eyes, he was standing there. Nicely I asked, "You always ruin my fun so what do you want, now?"

Having a serious expression he asked, "Don't you need to be home with our son and not out here at a place like this, dressed like that?"

"Don't you need to be in your son's life and not in a stepchild's life? Other words play daddy to your cum and not to another man's nut" was my response.

"You going to get somebody hurt just keep doing what you do."

"What is it that you think I am doing?"

In a distance, I saw Blackie's eyes. I wasn't in the mood for men to mark their territory, but I was pleased Blackie was on his way to my table. He came over and gave Ahmad the what's-up nod and asked me front of Ahmad, "Is this seat taken?"

Licking my lips, I sat up and said with a hard stare at Blackie, "It is, if you going to sit in it."

Making my glare at Ahmad then back to Blackie, I said "If not move out the way for the next man get it."

On that dark skinned man, those white teeth brighten as I became excited. I liked what I was seeing I waved my hand for him to sit. Ahmad strolled off with an attitude. Blackie smiled and said, "Did I ruin something?"

"You can't ruin what's already spoiled."

"Well said."

The waitress came over and he asked, "What you drinking?"

"What you buying?"

Blackie shook his head with a smile as he said, "The lady will have a Martini on ice and anything else she wants. I will have a Sex on a Beach with a twist and put it on my tab."

"Yes, Sir."

She walked off and my party crew came over and I said, "If you guys don't mind let us sit here."

The others said ok and walked off, but J Lamb said, "He the manager here, tell his ass to put us in the VIP section; that's if he can."

I glanced at him then asked, "Can you do that? I mean put us in a private section of this nice establishment?"

"I can do that and so much for you if you let me."

J Lamb spoke like he is my manager, "She didn't ask for that; you going too far too early in the game."

Leaning over to me he said, "Take his ass to the cleaners for everything" all I could do was smile.

"J Lamb, she is not like you so you can stop advising her to be you."

"Blackie, clarify your statement because I think you want sex tonight; that you ain't getting."

"J Lamb, it's not all about sex. She's not that type of bitch."

Quickly I butted in to say, "I'm a bitch because I desire a man to take his time to please me sexually? Or am I a bitch because I don't give a shit about what others think?"

Blackie didn't take long before he spoke, "The second one."

He got up and held his hand out to help me up like a man should. J Lamb spoke, "That's what I'm talking about."

As we were walking across the floor, Lovers and Friends began to play. Blackie did me a partial twirl as we began slow dancing. Not the type that caused us to be all on each other but the type that showed chemistry. At one point, I placed my back and allowed him to hold me as we romantically rocked to the music.

I didn't just bounce to the music of course; I made my body slow wave upon him. Being the gentleman, he held my hands and did a slow two step to me as we faced each other to dance to the music. Ever so calmly he pulled me close to him and placed his arms about my waist. I, on the other hand, placed my hands around his neck as we slow dance sexually.

He twirled me outward as he held my hands up above my head as to show me off. The spotlight is all on me as my stripper tease came out of me. The men that were dancing nearby were watching me because I made sure to be noticeable. Blackie kept flashing those pearly whites at me, and that made me put on a show for real.

He pulled me close and said, "They don't need to see what I'm watching. Get their own show, you mine."

The rest of the song, we held onto each other and swayed. Seconds later, a woman came over and interrupted us by saying, "Blackie."

He ignored her and this time she nearly pulled him off me to say, "Blackie."

I stopped and waited for him to respond. He looked at her and said, "What?"

"You know you fucking up right by being here with her, don't ya?"

"I'm a grown man. I do what I want to do."

I butted in and asked, "Is he your husband?"

"Ain't any of your business what he is to me?"

Giving my attention to him, I politely asked, "Is she your wife?"

"Hell, no. I'm legally separated from a wife that's not here."

Stepping to the woman I said, "He's with me tonight, and if he wants to leave, he's free to do so. Until then back the fuck up."

"Who you talking to like that?"

"There's two bitches standing here and one of us is confident and aggressive while the other one is insecure and a doo girl. Until you find out which one you are, get the hell out my way."

I took it that he was surprised at my tone for he said before the standoff took another route, "Ladies, its ok."

"Blackie, I'm walking off to the VIP. When you finish with trash put it in the garbage and hurry up because my time is precious and valuable."

I walked off not caring what she was saying to him. J Lamb came met me at the door of the VIP room and asked, "I thought I had to help you whip her ass."

"I don't need help."

"Good, I didn't feel like fighting no way. Glad y'all handled it like women."

"I don't think she knows that fronting on me about a nigga that doesn't belong to she nor I shows a sign of weakness."

"You studying people now?"

Giving a tender chuckle, I said "All I was doing was dancing."

"I thought y'all needed a room the way you were nasty dancing."

"It got men's attention, didn't it?"

"Women too; dykes here."

I laughed again and spoke, "Fuck them."

"Don't think they won't let you, acting like y'all the only ones in the building."

"That is how you do it. You tune everyone out and

make sure the man you with is getting your full attention or make him think he is but the entire time, you want the attention of all the men in the building."

"Like my brother?"

"Ahmad?"

"How many other brothers do I have?"

"I didn't pay him any attention."

"That is why he stormed out the place. The way you were grinding out there I thought you were preparing meat for seasoning."

Laughing I said, "Get me something to drink."

He handed me some of the liquor Blackie had ordered while we were on the floor. I went over to the balcony and J Lamb followed me. As we overlooked the crowd he said with an approval, "You are a strong bitch. I didn't say lady because she left when you did."

"I receive that."

"Wait we ain't at church and I wasn't prophesying."

Laughing I spoke, "Just because I am aggressive now and determined to be the best and look my best does not really make me uppity."

"Yes, it does."

He pointed to a group of women in the back of the

club as he whispered, "These hungry hoes here don't know what a real bitch is like. They think looking good, living off the government and being on the low makes them classy, but they trashy. They need to get some business."

By the door in the corner, I saw her. She had on booty shorts, a belly shirt and I couldn't see what were on her feet. The girl I had to get straight was amongst them. I asked J Lamb without removing my eyes from them "Isn't that the woman that came out the house when Ahmad came over?

"Yeah."

"Isn't she also the same one that came to my wedding, wearing a wedding dress?"

Speaking loudly with alto in his words, "Yeah, that's the bitch."

"Thought so."

I began to storm off and J Lamb asked as he trailed, "What you finna do?"

Before I could make it to the door, Blackie came. We stopped, and he asked, "Were you about to leave?"

"I was because you were taking too long to take your trash out."

J Lamb started laughing.

"I like you," Blackie said.

"You've already told me that. Tell me something else."

Looking at my best friend he spoke, "J Lamb, the next two rounds on me so bounce."

"Free drinks; enough said."

My best friend turned around and left me standing. I asked, "I want us to sit by the balcony and watch the people."

"Your wish is my command."

Blackie and I chose a seat like I asked. I needed a seat so she can see me, and I can see her.

"You having a good time?"

"I am, but I'm hungry now."

"Look at the menu, and I will get it over to you."

He handed me a menu, and I didn't see anything I really wanted so I just said, "How about appetizers of white cheese dip?"

"Want some wings to go along with it?"

"Why not, J Lamb might be hungry too?"

"This isn't for him."

"It's for anyone I want it to be. He is my best friend and if he doesn't eat I don't eat. So be nice when it comes to him. That is one way to piss this bitch off."

Flashing those teeth he smiled to say, "Ok, it's whatsoever you want. Let me make you happy."

"Thank you."

He had another waitress take our order. He and I talked and talked as we ate the appetizers. Sometimes, I would find myself letting my guard down and letting the nice caring me surface. Soon as I saw her arising out of her grave, I would bury her and let my new attitude show up.

Being in his company made me feel like a real woman as we danced and danced. His personality is warm, and his essence is that of a man that knows what he wants out of life. I was actually enjoying my evening. Out the corner of my eye I saw those women on the floor trying to dance all up on men. It was heartbreaking to see them try to do what I can do.

"Blackie, can I get on stage and make an announcement?"

"Tonight is your night. Do what you want."

He led me to the stage. The D.J. handed me the microphone. I said, "Put the spotlight on my girls in the back of the club."

Instantly the spotlight, went to the women that were by Ahmad. His face was that of what is going on. With a few drinks under my belt and a sober mentality to match I spoke, "I'm a bitch but not your average everyday bitch but a bitch with standards and class to match. Women you don't have to act; all you have to do is be like me and show the fuck up. Men if you want an assured woman that is getting hers look on this stage but if you want thirsty hoes that sweat other bitches about their game; go to the spotlight. I guarantee there is one or two in the bunch. Enjoy the rest of the night."

I walked off stage and Blackie said, "Who or what made you the way you are?"

"I was bitch made because another bitch shaped me into not holding in anything. And sometimes you can't help but to act like a bitch even if u don't want to be one. Many women blame society and environment, not understanding they are similar. In the core of it all, you can't be caring in a cruel world because it will get you in trouble. Don't blame me; blame the bitch that made me."

J Lamb came over and said, "You might have to claw your ass out here to the ride."

Shrugging my shoulders, I spoke "They don't want me tonight or any other night; I will fuck their world up."

Blackie touched my hand tenderly and said to my eyes, "You don't have to worry about that. You with me and no man or woman will fuck with you while I am around."

"Why, thank you, Blackie."

128

He kept watching me like a prize that I am, so I asked, "You going to take me home or what?"

J Lamb acted like he was possessed as he said loudly, "Hell, no, you know the routine. We come here together; we leave here together. So, if his ass is taking you home, his ass is taking all of us home."

"My Camaro isn't big enough for all of you."

J Lamb spoke as he snatched my hand form Blackie, "Guess her ass is riding with us."

I was in a trot behind my best friend as we went outside. The other guys had paired up with others and left. J Lamb took the keys and said, "Guess I'm the sober one to drive."

"You not driving me anywhere."

"Get your own keys. I can't be responsible for your shit anyway."

Taking the keys, I got in and when I switched on the lights, I saw Ahmad. He didn't appear happy. It bothered me and it shouldn't. Just for a brief instant we feasted your eyes on the other. My husband is tall, but he seems to have lost weight. The girl saw me in the vehicle and shoved him to move on.

He did and like a mechanism of a clock, I took in that he was still letting a bitch like her run him. J Lamb saw my gaze and spoke, "Girl, if you don't put this bitch in drive and run them the hell over; I will."

"You will go to jail."

"And if I do, you better come get me out."

"How about if they move and we drive on?"

"How about you give them some help."

J Lamb put his hands on the steering wheel, and the car went towards them. Ahmad did not move, but the rest of them did. In the rear-view mirror, I saw them standing and yelling at me.

"You could have hurt someone."

"Could of but I didn't. Get this vehicle to your crib, I'm hungry."

"You didn't eat at the club?"

"You didn't get any food."

"Yes, I did. Blackie bought white cheese dip and wings."

"That shit is for white people, but it sounds good right about now."

"I had him to buy it, but you didn't come by to eat."

"Ty, free liquor or dip and wings? You tell me which you think I choose."

130

"That is why you hungry now."

"That is why I am going to your house to eat."

I parked in my vehicle slot, and we got out. Right behind us was Ahmad and Bianca. She got out the car barking and not biting. J Lamb and I turned to see what the commotion was about. When she saw that I was looking, she dashed towards me, and Ahmad grabbed her. Yelling the words "Let her go. Let her find out if this is the ass she wants to fight."

"I'm going to get that ass!"

Screaming at Ahmad, I spoke "Let her go. If she wants this ass, here it is. It's not running, and it damn shole ain't hiding."

J Lamb being drama as usual, he yelled out to Ahmad, "Come on brother let her go. She has been running her mouth for over a year saying what she will do to Ty. Here Ty, there's Bianca, let her go."

Glaring back at J Lamb, I asked loud enough for Ahmad and her to hear, "She been running her mouth, you say?"

"Ty, when she ain't running her mouth. If I were you, I would teach her a lesson, breaking up your wedding and now laying up with your husband. I'll have to have that ass if I do say so myself."

"J shut up and keep Ty in her apartment and stop

instigating!"

"He doesn't have to take me anywhere. I'm a grown ass woman with the backbone of a bitch."

J Lamb whispered to me, "Act like you going to charge, and I'll hold you back."

I sprang into action and began to charge her. J Lamb snatched me up like he was picking me up. I kept hollering, "Put me down! Let me go! Let me get that home wrecker!"

J Lamb shouted, "Ahmad, I can't hold her much longer! She very feisty over here!"

Ahmad finally took Bianca in their place as J Lamb put me down, and we started laughing as we went to mine.

"You see the look on Ahmad's face?"

"I swore he thought it was real."

"He probably did at first, but he has seen that act from us before. He knows it was fake."

We laughed some more as we ate sandwiches and chips. It seemed like hours, but the sun was coming up, so we lay down. Sleep must not have been my friend long because J Lamb did not knock but he stormed in my room and jumped on my bed. I rose up with my hand upon my face to say, "It's too early."

"Girl, your ass all over Facebook."

The minute he said that I tried to open my eyes, but the sun's rays were blinding me.

"Close the blinds."

"Didn't nobody tell you to drink all they had last night. Wait that was me. But here, I'll close the blinds."

He closed the blinds, and I sat up in bed. He handed me a Sprite soda, and I tasted it. I placed the can on the nightstand and asked, "Now who's on Facebook?"

"You ass on Facebook, that's who."

"Let me see it. Who posted me on Facebook?"

"It's a fake page. Trust me, I tried finding out who did it but it don't matter, you have over two hundred likes."

"What am I doing?"

"That slutty dance."

He showed me on his Nook, and I could not believe it. It was damn good dance tease, if I must say so.

"What a way to wake up in the morning."

"Yo ass even got niggas commenting and wanting to know who you are."

"Really?"

"From the way you working it out, they wouldn't believe yo ass used to be fat."

"Every clique has a hating bitch and you mine" I stated to J Lamb.

"Somebody has to envy you from within."

"Has your brother seen it?"

J Lamb took his Nook from me and said, "He has now because I just tagged him in it."

"You drama-filled bastard."

"You didn't lose the weight and gained attitude just to keep it to yourself, did you?"

I didn't say a word as I grinned.

"Well, did you?"

"All this is a personal battle for me."

"Personal my ass, we in this together."

"Since when did I get a twin?"

"Since the day I met you in the ninth grade, that's when."

He was right. Since he became my friend, we have always been together in some form. On no account had J Lamb left my side. We have been best friends and as a team, with Ahmad included. We have all had our share of ups and downs. That is why I can't believe that the man I have loved is weak in some form.

Ahmad always tried to do the right thing and to him, he must assume that she needed him more than I did. With that thought I asked, "She might have done it."

"Girl ain't no telling; wouldn't put it past her or her friend."

"I don't know her friend."

"She the one you told Blackie to finish taking his trash to the garbage."

Giggling I asked with curiosity, "I sure did tell him that. How you know?"

"Bitches talk. They will tell everything until it's something to make them look stupid."

"You must talk to these bitches?"

"I don't have to talk to them. They talk to bitches I talk, too and those bitches tell my bitches and my bitches tell me."

J Lamb left out my room, and I laid there with thoughts of Blackie on my mind. That dark- skinned man is gorgeous to me. His swag is on point, and his company is awesome. The way he smiles at me makes me grin like a silly girl letting her crush knows she is into him.

For the first time, I was in bed thinking about a man other that Ahmad and it was creepy. So far we just cool, and I don't think he is that strong of a man to get and keep my mind off my husband, but who knows. I just might let him take some of this pressure off me.

CHAPTER 7

I got up and showered. Pastor Tatum called, but I did not answer because I knew he's going to ask about coming to church and I don't want to lie to him. Right after I put my clothes on, J Lamb came in the room talking on his cell. I was moving my head and my hands, no, but he cheerfully said, "Here she go, daddy."

Taking the phone from him, I gave him a stare. He said, "Well, he asked why you weren't answering your phone. I didn't want to lie to him; I wanted you to do it. Hurry up, he on mute."

Unmuting the phone, I gave a happier tone, "Good morning, Pastor."

"Good morning. I've been calling your cell, and I knew you two were together."

"I saw you called, then J Lamb came in and handed me the phone."

"This is a friendly reminder about service this morning, and how I haven't seen you since your return to the state."

"I won't be able to make it."

"Well, I will keep praying for you to come back. It's never too late, and I look forward in seeing you."

"I know."

"Alright."

We got off the phone and I said, "You always do that to me."

"You are always slipping."

"I'm going to get you one day."

That precise time a loud shattering rang out. We both went to the window and saw a woman knocking out the back glass of Blackie's Camaro. We faced each other and took off towards the living room. She spun off. I was going in case she tried to break my glass out. I asked, "Who was that?"

"Blackie's legally separated wife slash woman slash girlfriend slash stalker slash the bitch that will get your ass for being with her husband."

"With all those titles, she better have more than just a want for this ass?"

"Yup, it depends on what she is this week."

We laughed. Blackie came out the house wearing pajamas and no shirt to see what happened and so did we and all the neighbors. Instantly, he saw his car window and was totally pissed. He started looking around for answers, but no one said a word. I didn't blame him for being angry. Those windows are expensive, and that's a new car.

Blackie saw me and came over. He grinned and oddly enough, his demeanor changed when he said, "I can't stand childish women."

"Why she do that?"

J Lamb added, "Do you need to ask or you having a blond moment?"

"Her sister went back and told her about us being together."

"And?"

"And she saw the video post of you dancing while I held your hand in the air."

J Lamb put his sense in by saying, "Imagine what she gone do when you give it to him."

"Nothing but sit down somewhere."

Blackie said, "You gonna give it to me?"

Concentrating was hard to do when you have a nice-looking man in front of you. Not only is that, but his smile is one that will make you weak, if you are weak. The way his chest looks and how he smells made me cheese like a child. J Lamb pushed me and said, "You want her to give it to you, I'll talk to her and."

I cut him off and said, "Shut up with your lying self."

He gave me that fake face as he said, "I'm trying to help you out."

"If he gave you an open tab in the VIP I'm done."

"Right but that's not the point."

Blackie said, "You want me to have, what you want to give?"

"Depends if you act right but right now, we crawling."

"Let's crawl then."

J Lamb said, "First, you need to handle your business. I don't need my prime investment to be caught up in bullshit because you can't keep your hoes in check."

"He has a point," I added.

"The only thing you need to worry about is smiling and what I can do to make that happen."

Ahmad came out the house dressed for service alone. J Lamb yelled out, "You can't speak brother?"

He shook his head and put his hands up as a form of not verbally speaking. He got in the car and backed out. Before putting it in drive, he gave me an unsatisfied gesture. I didn't like it, but I respected it.

"I have to get ready for service."

"I thought you weren't going?" J Lamb asked with a straight face.

"You misunderstood. I said I was going because afterwards I can see my family."

As if to poke holes in my story he said, "No. I specifically thought I heard you tell daddy that you can't make it today."

"You were eavesdropping too hard."

"Is that what I was doing? I swear you have speech impairment because what you just said was nothing like I heard you tell your dear old Pastor."

"You were eavesdropping too hard" I stated again.

Letting me off the hook, J Lamb stated "Ok, I was listening too hard."

Blackie asked, "Can I see you later on this evening?"

"Maybe."

"Maybe?"

"Yes, maybe because Boss bitches have shit to do and plans do vary."

"Ok. When you become available, text me or call me; as long as I get a chance to hear from you today."

"Will do."

My best friend and I left him standing there looking after us. Soon as we got in the house I ran for J Lamb, but he locked himself in my son's room. He knew I was coming after him because he almost got me caught up, but I squirmed away nice and clean.

Forgetting all about him, I went and changed clothes. I know Josiah will be at service with my brother and his family and right now, family time is what I need. Deciding on a nice Sunday church dress, I put on a pair flat to match. I came out and J Lamb was standing at the door and said, "I'm ready."

"Where you going?"

"You think I am going to let you go alone to serve the Lord?"

"Lets' go and where you get the clothes from?"

"I always have a backup bag."

"With church clothes in it?"

"Let's see, I went out on a Saturday night and today is Sunday. I just assumed church will be today for me. You only going because my brother is going."

"My car, my gas, my business."

Rushing me to the door, J Lamb stated, "Let's go Ty we running late."

I locked my door as we left in my vehicle. Turning the station to gospel, J Lamb said, "Naw pop that booty; put it back on that."

"We on our way to church so we need some Godly music."

"You right, it's good to be phony for one day."

"While we in line I hope you get delivered."

"Speak for yourself. I'm not getting in the prayer line. He gonna call you and Ahmad watch my talk. As for getting delivered daddy gone have to come with it because I have a lot of demons lined up. They aren't going to leave this house so easily."

That was not funny although, he does have demons like that. I just continued driving and thought about seeing Ahmad. The more I drove I recalled how I decided on spending all my time making my husband see what he was missing in his real family. Quite often enough people don't know what they miss until it is too late and when a woman has expertise at being a bitch, she can make him do just about whatsoever she wants.

The truth of the matter is, men like bitches and not just that, the bitch has to have her stuff together. And that was what I did. I saw how he protected her and how she still runs him. The power she has over him is mine and I want it back.

"Stop dreaming about making that hardheaded brother of mine listens to you. If I could and I will, she will pay for the things she has done to you both and everyone else."

"We here."

This is the first time I have been to this church since I

tried to kill myself. I sat there when I parked the car. J Lamb asked, "You going to be ok?"

"I have faith I will be."

"If it's of any help I am really here for you."

Turning to face my best friend, I felt self-assured for he was genuine. He knew how distraught I was on my wedding day and how other events in my life has tested me. Through it all, he as always remained true, even when Ahmad didn't.

"Jamal that means so much to hear you say that. It is hard for me to go back inside and face some of those people that were there, but I must."

"Do what you have too. I got you. You my best friend and when your best friend aches so do you. If those old hags want some gossip, I will give them something to gossip about."

"What about Ahmad, he's your best friend, too?"

"He is my best friend but he just stupid ain't no other way around it. My brother puts the S in stupid."

Laughter filled my car as he said, "Let's get out and let them know that some bad."

Cutting him off I yelled, "No, we at church."

"I see now this is going to be one of those days, and we need to hurry the heck up and leave."

I locked the doors with the switch. Once we made it to the foyer, I froze. The last time I was at these doors, I was about to walk down the aisle.

"It's ok. I got you" J Lamb whispered to me as the Usher opened the doors for us.

Some faces were familiar as the seats in the back were inviting. Pastor Tatum saw us. Taking in inventory, I didn't see Jessica or the children; therefore, I knew Josiah was at home with Jessica and I was cool with that. Ahmad was not seen. Then out of the back, he came. He saw me and made his way towards me. He stared at me, and I wanted to cry but refused to do so. I listened as Pastor preached on what it means to do right. Personally, it's a message his son needs to get and was not.

Then the alter call was called. I sat there and looked back at J Lamb. He was on the back seat asleep, but if you didn't know better you would think he was deep in prayer as his head was in his hands. Someone called my name, and it was Pastor Tatum. I didn't want to get up. The Usher came and said, "Pastor wants you to come up front with your husband."

Being obedient, I got up and stood by Ahmad. "Hold hands."

He and I stared at each other, and my brother took our hands and placed them inside each other before anointing our head. Pastor Tatum spoke between us so surrounding people could not hear. "I know you two still have love for each other, and the enemy has worked his way in this marriage but today, we want to pray for your strength as a family unit. It's not just for you both, but for that little boy you both cherish dearly. He needs his parents to come together to raise him strong and mightily. Josiah can't have that if his parents let outside forces dictate how they are to do things. You two are married and sooner or later you're going to have to face it. Think about the love you have, and the son you both love so much."

My brother Josh placed blessing oil on our foreheads. I glanced back at J Lamb, and he put his head down, in fear that his dad would call him for prayer. I thought he would have done his favorite by going to the bathroom, but he didn't. Pastor Tatum said, "Lift your hands." He put one hand on Ahmad's forehead, and the other one on our conjoined hand. I closed my eyes like Ahmad did.

Pastor said a few words and Ahmad fell. Being that he had my hand, I fell with him. I didn't know what was happening, but I saw the feet of J Lamb trotting out the door in a hurry. They put a sheet over Ahmad, and I got up. I got up and made my way outside. I saw J Lamb sitting on the bench by the tree. I went to him, and he was closing his cell phone.

I asked, "Why you leave?"

"My demons didn't want him to cast them out. I don't have time today to be purging and carrying on."

"You silly."

146

"You saw the way Ahmad went out? Then you fell down. It was a matter of time before he was calling me. I figured he can't call what he can't see. That is why I left."

"I went down because he was holding my hand."

"Oh, I thought you done got the Holy Ghost or something. I was about to catch me another ride to get my car from your crib."

Not able to contain my laughter, I asked "You about ready?"

"I am, but you have a visitor coming this way."

"Who?"

"Don't look, but it's your hubby."

Ahmad looked at J Lamb and asked, "Let me talk to Ty."

"I guess so. She your wife not mines."

J Lamb walked off as Ahmad said, "I want you to know that I did not plan this."

"I know you didn't. Your dad has a mind of his own."

An awkward moment occurred as he asked, "You seeing Blackie now?"

"Why are you asking about my social life?"

147

"I do still love you, Ty."

"I think you need to lay back down and let God finish dealing with you because you out here telling me you love me."

In a swift move Ahmad, twirled me to him and hugged me tightly. I swore he closed his eyes and for a moment he acted like he remembered how we use to be. I only stood there not knowing how to take this. He finally let me go and said, "I had to feel you in my arms again. I never meant to hurt you. I only did what I thought was right. I thought that I made a mistake and have to correct it, but it was worse than I thought."

I cut him off and demanded, "Don't. I don't want to hear it. You had all the time in the world, but you didn't. Excuse my Sunday language, but I'm all out of fucks to give today, but if you come back tomorrow one maybe found, next week for sure."

Walking off from him as fast as I could was the only option. I heard him calling after me, but I don't want to hear anymore lies from him. Luckily, service was over, and I saw my brother and thought about going to see Jessica. She would look at me and know something was wrong. I have known Jessica all my life. She and my brother Josh have been together for too many years and that makes her the sister I never had.

I can talk to her privately but if she feels the need to tell Josh she will. They are married and secrets are not of

God; therefore, if I don't want Josh to know I better not tell her. Today is one of those days. I don't want to hear any reason for Ahmad telling me he still loves me. I just didn't care to hear it.

Saying goodbye to my brother, I threw J Lamb the keys; he said, "You must be delirious because you throwing me the keys to the Range Rover. Whatever it is, you need to feel like it more often."

J Lamb got in the driver seat. I sat there staring out the window before I asked, "Is your brother the dumbest guy this side of the state or what?"

"We talking about Ahmad, right?"

"Who else?"

"You know he dumb. I tried telling you when I introduced you, but, no, you wouldn't listen."

"Really, J Lamb?"

"Yeah, all you kept saying was, I love him, I love him, oh how I love your brother and look at your love for him now? It's with another woman."

"Why you do that?"

"Do what?"

"Tell me about Ahmad and tell him about me?"

"Y'all are my best friends. What kind of friend will

I be if I didn't tell my best friend what the other friend is doing?"

J Lamb turned the radio off gospel and put on some slow jams.

"I know what the problem for you is Tiger."

"You a doctor now?"

"I did know some white coats."

"Ok, what is my problem?"

"You need new dick in your life. Dick period."

I laughed as we pulled into the apartment. We got out and I asked, "When you ever going back to work?"

"You know they fired my ass. Why you think I said did know some white coats?"

"For real? I thought you were speaking in past tense as if you had a new job lined up."

"Yeah, they say I can't come to work on time, and I am not dependable."

"Are you? I can answer that for you."

"Just because I supposed to be there at six and I come at ten doesn't mean anything. If they piss in the bed, they better wait until I get there. It's not my fault if they have to lay in it until the help comes."

Looking at him I laughed as I opened the door. I didn't make it in good before my cell started ringing. It was Blackie. The text read: You free to go to the park for a picnic?

"J Lamb, Blackie wants to take me out to the park."

"Well go. It's not like my brother is going to take you."

Texting back: When?

Blackie: In an hour. Got a surprise for you.

Me: Ok.

"He's coming in an hour."

"What you going to wear?"

"Something that says I am a conservative."

"Conserving what, energy? Last time I checked that was an act passed in Washington years ago to get energy to rural America."

"I just can't win with you. You always have something to say."

"But I give you facts."

Going to my room, I freshened up. Deciding to wear my hair up and no makeup, I put on a quarter sleeve blouse with my cleavage peeking out the top and a long skirt. I came out and J Lamb's mouth fell open as he spoke, "You went in a sinner and now you a sinner saint. You gonna confuse him because you are confusing me right now."

"You like this?"

"The question is will he like it because last night you were dressed like a hoe and now you done gone to a churchy hoe."

A knock was heard at the door. I opened the blinds a little and saw it was Blackie. Not just that, but he had flowers. Dressed like he was carefree made me glad of the choice I picked up. Behind him was a black, Chrysler 300. My heart moved rapidly. I whispered to J Lamb, open the door."

He screamed, "You open it. Your house, your door."

I spoke, "Ok, when I get back be gone out of my house and lock my door."

"Girl, since you put it like that, let me get that door. You know I was playing."

He opened the door, and Blackie smelling just as good as the flowers said, "Here" without looking at the person at the door.

"These ain't for me. I ain't your bitch."

Blackie looked up into J Lamb's face. Blackie spoke, "J Lamb, you know they aren't for you and if you were my bitch I will trade up."

"Oh, we will see."

Turning to me J Lamb asked, "Where these go, in the garbage inside or outside?"

"Cut it out."

"I'm just asking."

"In the vase on the table."

"Next to those dried up ones or what?"

Shaking my head, I gave Blackie a hug and said, "Are you always a gentleman?"

"Only in the presence of a real independent woman."

Hollering from the kitchen, J Lamb said, "Well you need to leave those hood rats alone."

"We gone."

Blackie was standing at my side of the door. Ahmad came out and stared at me. Bianca and Brian came out. He locked the boy inside and rolled his eyes at me. Blackie asked with a tease, "You getting in this car or that one?"

"I guess this one because I don't think your sister would let me ride in that one."

He let me in, and he got in. I said, "You see Ahmad roll his eyes at me?"

"He just being childish and don't want a real man to be the man to the woman he married."

He pulled off as I said, "I like that answer."

"What park we going to?"

"You pick."

"The one by Louisville High School."

"Ivy?"

"I think."

"Perfect."

As we began our journey I asked, "When you getting your window fixed?"

"Early next week."

"What about your woman slash separated wife, slash girlfriend or what she is to you this week?"

Laughing he said, "She knows I have my interest elsewhere and she can't take it."

"You do?"

"She had me and she didn't want me. I gave her anything she asked for and still she was not satisfied. There was nothing else left for me to do. I could not make her happy and it took a while for me to get the concept that you can't make someone happy if they don't want to be happy."

"I know that hurt."

"It did but I decided that I needed to live. I didn't want to go through my life without saying that I didn't try. I at least want to do my all before giving up on a woman I called my wife."

"She didn't see it that way, did she?"

"No, but the saddest part is, she knew that I would wait for her because I have done it for so long. That day I saw you at the place you in now, I knew that waiting on her was over and if she didn't want to be with me so be it. I've done my part of being a good and faithful husband."

"Well, she better not come at me with that bullshit."

"She may want to just to scare you off because she has done it in the past before."

"She can say what she wants. If she jumps stupid, it's right back at her and she may not like what I say to her."

"I hope you are a keeper. Right now, as a friend you are what I am looking for."

"I hope so."

"Ty, you won't have to worry about anything. When I am with you, I am with you; I got you."

"All I have to worry about are other women, and worrying is the least I am going to do."

"Be you and keep it real; she didn't."

"She sounds like a fool to me, if I ever did hear of one."

"Just like Ahmad but their loss maybe our gain. He should have made it work with you."

"If he had, then you wouldn't be here with me."

"Point well taken" he said as he smiled those teeth at me.

I forgot all about his crazy wife. As long as she stayed in her place and realize her problem is not with me, we will be cool. If she loses sight of that her problem will be mine and real bitches don't do drama. Calmly I said, "You leading her on?"

"Hell, no. I wish we could get things straight because she is a good girl."

"Well, your good girl better know that right now we are good friends and you in the company of a better girl."

"I heard that."

Being flirty, I responded, "You better."

As he turned into the park, Blackie said "How about if we don't discuss him or her for that matter?"

"Who you talking about again?"

He saw the direction I was going so he laughed. I

stopped laughing when I saw Ahmad's car. Blackie said, "We can go somewhere else if you want?"

"No, I'm not going anywhere. He has his life, and I am getting mine."

Blackie parked the car a few feet shy from his. My date opened my door and extended his hand for me to take. I took it and gave him the smile I only gave Ahmad. Blackie handed me the sheets and tablecloth. He picked up the basket. We walked to the table under the covered area. Bianca was there watching her son in the child's swing five feet away.

She spoke to her brother and turned her head when she laid eyes on me. She acts like I owe her when she has my husband. Ignoring her, Blackie placed the sheets on our seats and put the tablecloth on the table. He unpacked the Subway sandwiches and wine. I saw Ahmad looking at me, and I smiled. He got out and strolled towards us.

Bianca said, "You hungry, baby?"

Ahmad mumbled, and she said, "Go get Jr. out the swing."

He looked at me, and I hid my displeasure. He didn't say anything but did as she asked of him. I comprehended the game from her point of view because it's a language that only bitches understand. Ahmad came back with the little boy, and I knowingly asked Blackie, "You didn't pack the dessert and that is the best part of any meal."

157

"As if you didn't know, you are my dessert, and I can't wait to sample it."

Ahmad frowned as I took notice how his hands ball into a fist as he heard that. I liked it and to win I went with the flow. "You just want a sample and not the whole thing?"

"A sweet tooth is after I've had the whole thing a time or two."

Blackie and I laughed, but I laughed hysterically. Ahmad said something to Bianca as he walked off to the car. I know that bothered him, but if he wants to take it there, we will go there. She gave me a stare off. I stood up and motioned the "what you want to do look" as to fight. Ahmad called after her. She got her son, and they left.

"Don't let her get to you; she's just mad because you have more power than you think."

"Where were we?" I asked to forget about them.

We were alone, and it was nice. The wind was polite as the sun played peek a-boo with the clouds. The wine was kicking in with the anticipation of sex was escalading. I was feeling loose and stirred. The mood was right. I sensed it, and so did he. We would talk with our eyes when we kept our conversation to a minimum.

However, the more we talked and laughed the more the mood was right. He is nice and wants to have a family, which is a plus. He hasn't rushed me and is willing to wait until I am ready. There is no denying, I want him. If we keep this up, there will be no turning back. Although the day was changing, so was my mind frame.

The sun was about to set within another two hours. The wind was beginning to be cool as he reached up and touched my chin. Taking my head, I held his hand between my face and shoulders. Softly he rubbed my jaw and spoke, "We better go."

CHAPTER 8

Things were beginning to wind down for us. I had never laughed so much in my life. Blackie was a comedian as he told me jokes and funny stories. Today going with him was the best decision I had made. The company was what I needed, and I wasn't disappointed.

From time to time he would, wipe a food particle from my mouth and each touch recapped my mind in what I was missing. This man was making my day, and I was not going to be a fool and not delight myself in it. His manners were excellent, and the way he was making me feel was running a close second.

In essence, this woman's husband is working a number on me. He is winning with me and doesn't even know it. It is women like his wife that are not strong enough to take what he has to give. Blackie is poised and knows the type of women he searches for; it just so happens to be me right now.

In a split second, I discerned his intent as he cupped my face. I didn't close my eyes for I didn't want that to happen. I haven't had time to see just what he is willing to do for me when it comes to the other women, I know he may have. Out of nowhere, he said "I want to take you somewhere."

"You are taking me somewhere, if you aren't conscious enough to see it."

"All that will be in due time."

"What physical place are you talking about?"

"It's a surprise if you want to go."

"I won't go to Hell, and I won't go to Hell."

He laughed and stated, "Well, I don't plan to take you to Hell."

"That being said, I am down."

"When you are alone with me, you are the sweetest thing ever and sometimes you can be a handful."

"You either going to handle it or let another man handle it."

"That is what you said at the club, but I believe I am enough man for you Ty. You just have to let me show you."

"You have a wife."

He cut me off to add, "A wife that is legally separated with no ties."

"Yeah, but she must have something for her to come to your house and knock your window out."

"Trust me it is nothing."

"I was waiting for her to come across the parking lot in my living room waiting on her to mess with mine."

"She wasn't going to do that" Blackie added.

"She may not but I know that in order for a woman to act up you must be telling her something of still fucking with her. Which one is it?"

"Neither. She doesn't want me to find anyone, but she has gone over with her life, and there is no need for her to hold onto me. Do you want a divorce?"

"I do and I don't. Unlike you, he and I have a son. By that, I think there could be some hope" I needed to say.

"Believe there is some hope, or you want it to be some hope?"

"Both I guess, but Ahmad isn't giving me any problems."

"He may not tell it to you, but he is telling it to somebody. You don't think he knows how good of a woman you are, and he sees how I want you like many other men do?"

"He can tell it to who he wants as long as keeps it to himself."

Blackie touched my hand, and an electrical current flooded me. It caused me to jerk my hand away. Like a charm, he flashed those white teeth at me, and I liked it. At this point, I wanted him to kiss me, but I wasn't sure if I was ready for that to happen, just yet.

"You felt that didn't you?"

I only smiled, for the sensation has been there since the day I saw him at my place.

"You don't have to say anything because I felt it, too. Strange enough, we have chemistry, and we can either act on it or let it ride. Personally, I want to see how far we can go with this."

"Right now, I want to go slow. It will be stupid for us to jump into this, and we both are in a marriage. I need to know if the man that will be in my life can stand up for me when it comes to bullshit. If he can't defend me, how can I expect him to protect me when the need be?"

"Ty, I will protect you and you won't have to worry about my soon to be ex-wife. You make me smile with your attitude, and the way you don't keep anything back lets me know that you are an assured woman."

"Feels good to be taken as being real and not for granted."

Standing to his feet, he asked "You ready?"

We began to pack up the material. He folded the sheets for me as he did the tablecloth. He was smiling at me when this car rushed in. Both of us turned our heads, trying to figure out who it was. Two women got out. The driver had her cell phone out, one to assume to catch this action as the other lady stormed out the passenger side.

From the look on her face, I knew it was his separated wife. The knife was still on the table because the arrival of the guest delayed us. From her demeanor, she may want drama. But I am ready. I don't have to worry about fighting because that is what the man is for, but I will filet her ass, if she gets in my personal space.

Blackie saw her and spoke, "You brought her name up, and here she is."

The jealous wife didn't come too close to me, but she stopped short in arms reach of her husband to say, "What you doing here with this arrogant bitch?"

Being stern and doing what he supposed to, he checked her, "Stop the name calling and leave us alone. We aren't bothering you."

I knew then she needs a woman like me to verbally let her know what her place is. Nicely with a hint of bitch I retorted, "Thank you, glad you can identify a good bitch when you see one because the one in your mirror isn't it."

"I wasn't talking to you. I was talking to my husband but if I want your input, I will ask for it."

"You came here where I'm at. Evidently you know there is a reason he's here with me and not with you. So, if he is your husband you need to wonder why your husband is on a date with another woman."

She charged at me, but Blackie stopped her as he yelled at her to shut up. I didn't flinch as I stood there with a smile. Placing my hands on my hips, I taunted her with my words, "There must be something about the dick to make you come here."

Allowing her to see my eyes rake over Blackie, I continued, "I might need to discover what the dick is all about. What you think about that Blackie? Will I be able to find out how good the dick is?"

"You need to sit your dog ass down and work on your own marriage."

"I need to do a lot of things and at the top of my list is fucking your husband. Blackie, my cat is purring; you ready to pet her?"

His wife, peeped from around him to say, "Take that bitch to the pound, for a new owner because the one you wanting is taken."

"Blackie, I am ready to go; this begging bitch needs some business that I don't have time to give it to her."

"You won't be able to hide from me when I get my hands on you."

Out stretching my arms, I stated as positive and loud as I knew how by saying, "Hide? Bitch please. I don't run either but to let you know where I may be later, you can find me in your husband's bed with my legs wrapped all around him; giving him what he knows is good."

She and Blackie continued to have their own words as I walked over to her friend with the video cam, pointing my finger at his wife I said, "Facebook, Twitter, Insta-Gram, if you don't want a boss bitch like me to be in your shit; get on your shit. If you do, you won't have to run after dick; it'll run after you. Seeing the way, she chasing that dick, is proof. Be good Faces, Twit, Gram, I'm out."

Going back to the table, I picked up the sheets. Walking by her so she can try and put her hands on me, I strolled and said, "Blackie, when you finish with your dog, have it spayed and neutered; we don't need any more problems this evening and make it quick. I don't plan to stand outside long."

His wife tried to hit me. I stared at her and laughed in her face. She kept telling him how he doesn't need to be here with me. On the other hand, he kept telling her to go home so they can talk about it later. She kept talking to him. It was a pathetic scene as I waited outside the car for him to open the door.

Blackie was furious as he marched in front of her and opened the door for me. His wife yelled out, "We'll meet again!"

Insulting her by smiling, I placed the sheets in the back as I got in the car. Gently, he shut the door, and as they drove off, he got in.

"You, ok?" I asked.

"I'm ok. Just hate when she does this. It never fails, Tygeria. She finds where I am at and makes a scene. Just like that, she shows up and tries to do damage. Sometimes I wish she would get a life."

166

"Don't worry about her, I don't."

Before leaving he asked coyly, "Why you taunt her so? You know she is only going to act up again."

"No, she won't. She is going to reconsider her actions and get it right because a new bitch is on the scene."

He was about to drive off as he asked, "You still want me to show you the surprise?"

"Yeah, why wouldn't I?"

"I just thought you wanted to go home because she came."

Allowing my eyes to scan his body, I spoke "No. You said you have something for me, and I want it."

That smile on his face, lit what was dark as I spoke, "You know what you are doing when you smile like that to me. That's probably why she is acting up. You got her gone crazy."

He only grinned as he began to drive off. We stopped at the Dollar General in Noxapater. Blackie saw one of his employees with their hood up. While he was attending to them, I got out and went in the store. Picking up some Hershey's small candy, I went to the register. The girl stared at me as she asked, "You Tygeria Tatum?"

"Yeah, why?"

"I'm Devin's fiancé."

"So, what does that have to do with me?"

"I saw the way he was checking you out at the club and I want to let you know that he is about to be married."

"If there is something wrong with the way he was doing me, you need to check him and not me."

"I was just letting you know."

"Let yourself know. If he is giving you insecurities before the wedding imagine when you do marry him. Looks like a life of checking women that don't need to be check. Now you can check me out or call someone else. I don't have any more time to waste on a girl talking about a guy; whom I think is slow."

She didn't like that, but she took my money. I gave her a grin, looked her up and down as I proceeded out the door. Blackie was standing by the car waiting on me. He opened the door, and I got in asking, "You get them taken care of?"

"No, they said someone was coming for them."

"They could have gotten in here with us."

"No, they couldn't. Where he going to sit?"

"There is a back seat."

"Then where the basket and sheets going to be at?"

It was funny. He continued, "I'm on a date with a

woman and don't need an audience."

"You right about that. Who knows what they may see."

Flashing me those pearly whites made me lose my train of thoughts. We got to the four way stop and he took a left. We crossed the train tracks, and he continued driving as he asked, "You always have to have the last word when you are telling what you think?"

"Men want women to shut up all the time, but you can't shut a real superior bitch up. I have to make sure you get what I am expressing, so we can be on the same page."

"Ok."

We arrived to this huge hill. I cut my eye at him because I don't know why we are at a hill. Parking the car in the small parking area, he got out the car and opened the door for me. He prompted himself in front of the car to say, "People always talk about Black History but what about the history of the Choctaw and Chickasaw Indians? What about their contributions? They were slaves, too, and not just that, this Mound is a very important part in the history of Nanih Waiya and Winston County altogether."

I'm sure he did not see my face. Not really caring about what he was talking about. I pretended because we have a connection. Moving closer to him, I got in front of him and leaned back on him. He placed his warm arms around me. He held me as we stared at the huge hill.

169

The wind was blowing harder now. Blackie said, "If it wasn't late, I would take you up those steps so you can have a better view."

Turning around to face him, I said "A sentimentalist, I like that."

"You do?"

"Yeah, I do."

"What else you like?"

Reaching up I kissed him with ease. Returning the light contact I pulled back. He stared into my eyes and kissed me again, this time with more passion. I could taste the wine as the passionate moment was taking place. I pulled back and he cupped my face with his massive hands.

No man has done that since Ahmad. I was feeling guilty. Taking charge was one thing, but nothing has ever occurred between me and any man. Here I am taking pleasure in another man's kisses because I hadn't had this touch in over a year. Clouding my mind was the trail of kisses, Blackie was making on my neck. The way his lips brushed my skin was pleasurable and nowhere near sloppy.

If anything, they were the kind you would expect from a man that was experienced at making a woman aware that she is a woman in need. He said, "Every time I touch you, I have the urge to touch you more. If a man isn't careful, he will be addicted to what you have."

Shutting him up, I kissed him with fever. I didn't think I could stop this high he was taking me on because either the alcohol was talking, or my hormones were speaking for me. If any moment was right, this was it. Our breathing was rapid, and our touching became that of an eager person.

Blackie was making me right for the picking and he was plucking my flowers one layer at a time. The lights of a car broke up the engagement. We kind of hid our faces as the passerby screamed, "Get a room!"

The car went out of sight. The sun was down now. Blackie asked, "Should we do what they demanded?"

"Talking about getting a room?"

"If you want me and not your husband?"

"Why you say that?"

"I don't want to be second to no man. I know all Ahmad has to do is wake up from this dream he's in and what we have will just be a memory."

He was right to an extent, but I must cool off and become levelheaded again. Snuggling closer I said, "We both need to calm down and wait because when you get it, you won't let it go. All I ask is that you don't do anything underhanded."

"Ty, you have my word."

"If you lie, your word won't mean shit to me when you need it to count the most."

Blackie let me back in the car, and we drove off. This time we didn't say much because I don't need him to complicate my life by having sex. Laying my head on the seat to face him, I watched him. He is what a woman likes me need, but he is not what a woman like me loves; not right now. The way he pays attention to every detail is wonderful, and who knows, I thought.

He saw me watching him and he smiled.

"You don't need to do that. You might reignite the fire you started at the Mound."

"I might want to do that."

Showing him a smile, I turned my head to face the other side of the car. He placed his massive hands on my thigh, and it was like lava in my veins. I squirmed, and he smiled and removed his hand from me.

We made it back to my place, and it was packed. Someone must be having a house party. He got out and opened the door for me. A slow jam was playing when coiled me in his arms. Ahmad was watching us, and I had to make it count. Leaning into his embrace more, I allowed him to hold me.

Soon as the song was over, he walked me to the door, and we hugged. Ahmad kept his eyes on Blackie to make sure he didn't enter my house, and he didn't. J Lamb was more likely at the party, and I didn't care to be disturbed by anything else other than my thoughts.

I went to work the next day with joy. Flowers were everywhere for me, and everyone was being curious and wanted to know who was sending them. The only thing they had on them was just because you are you. I told J Lamb that Blackie was pampering me with these unexpected gifts, and I loved it. A man was giving me the attention I needed and deserved and with Ahmad watching me, it was all worth it.

CHAPTER 9

I hadn't seen Ahmad at work, but I know he knows I am there. A few weeks had passed, and I still saw no progress with Ahmad. Blackie and I are getting to know each other, but that is as far as I was allowing it to go. I don't believe I am ready for Ahmad to see me with another man; although, he has another woman. My morals are unchangeable and to be honest to have someone other than my husband is scary.

Every day I go to work in hopes to have Ahmad talk to me, but nothing. The attention I am getting is great, but I need to up it more. Ahmad is not giving me the response I thought he should. It's like I am trying to get him to mess up on her like he did me. So far it was not working. Her hooks must be deep rooted into my husband for nothing was breaking him. I could not stir an attitude out of him, much less a long look my way.

Wholeheartedly, I took this job just to force him to see me or have dealings with me; I have to readjust my ways. This morning, I got up and put on my high heels and a short dress that comes to my knees. Making sure, the dress was loose at the bottom and tight on the breast. I placed about my neck the necklace, Ahmad bought me when we first got together. Licking my lips with a gloss, I decided to tie my hair in a bun, to make me look more desirable than ever.

Soon as I parked my all black out, Range Rover,

Ahmad was walking across the street. He saw me and stopped walking and so did his friends. I could not believe my luck. He is watching me for the very first time, in a long time. Not only was he mesmerized; so were his friends. They were all staring so I pretended that I didn't see them.

Giving them something to look at, I walked with a seductive sway. By lunch half his friends had come into the office wanting some type of form or asking silly questions. I didn't mind. I was being me, flirty, but innocently sweet. The other women that worked in the office didn't like it, but I didn't care.

They don't do shit for me, and they aren't me. If they want attention, then they need to dress better than what they are. Then again, they won't help. They are up in age and dress older. More power to them, I'm going to do me and enjoy it. Lunch time came, and I called Jessica to check on my little man.

I talked to Josiah for a few minutes, but he was having so much fun with his aunt and uncle, I told him I will be by the weekend to get him. My family wants to keep him during the week while I work. I was fine with that because I didn't have a sitter. The thought of taking him to Mrs. Howard's Child Care crossed my mind but haven't done my research.

I needed to hear my song. Placing on my headphones, I played an old tune. Oddly enough, I put that choir voice to work. I was singing, and I know I sound good as I sang to my favorite tune. It's my lunch break, and I had about twenty minutes before I was due back, so I decided to walk through the small break room.

This was something I had not prepared to do, but I have to make my presence known as well as felt. Ahmad did not see me, but his friends did. I acted like I was in my own world as I opened the door with my eyes on the floor so I would be as if I didn't see them. I knew my husband was watching me, along with the other men.

Soon as I began singing, my body got a mind of its own. I was popping in a slow grind as I moved to the rhythm. Taking my money out as I looked at the snack machine like I was really into singing, dancing, and buying food. I was putting on a show like never before.

Must admit, I had taken up strip tease dancing when my weight shed so I knew how to tease a man and make them think about me. This instructor taught me how to ignore my environment and feel the beat with my body. Today I was thankful I learned what she was teaching.

I got my snack slow as I continued to bounce to the beat. Without looking at them, I acted as if they weren't real. I opened the other door and went out the door. I could still feel their eyes on me as I bounced out of sight. The rest of the day went by wonderful. From the scene, I put on Ahmad will be getting in touch with me.

When four o'clock came I was out the door. My cell went off, and it was my husband just like I thought. His text had no words but an angry red emotion face. I didn't text back. Getting into my ride, I stopped at Fred's. Before I could let the window up and open the door to get out, Ahmad was standing at my door.

He crouched over by placing his hands on top of my window so I could not let it up. I glanced up at him and spoke nicely, "You are blocking my exit."

He still did not say a word. I know he was mad, but I pretended not to notice as I spoke, "You blocking my exit by standing in front of my door. Please move."

Pain was in his eyes as he stated to me, "You lucky I don't do more than that."

"What's your problem?"

"Ty, what you trying to prove?"

Unknowingly I asked, "What are you talking about?"

He kept staring at me as if I could read his mind. I used to but since my wedding day I am unsure how he is and what he thinks. Ahmad said, "You know this isn't you. You know this person I see is not the woman I know. You have changed. You have a new look and attitude to go along with it, and it bothers me."

"Bothers you? I'm a bitch in the midst of bitches, so don't tell me what a bitch does bother you."

"Do you even pray anymore like you use too?"

"Do you know how to be honest anymore, like you use too?" I questioned him back with attitude.

"Well Ty, I've said what I had to say. You are not bad as you put on."

"You may think I am not bad; then again what bitch isn't?"

"What happened to the sweet you that went to church and stayed humbled? What happened to the woman I loved since the ninth grade?"

"She grew up and became a woman scorned by a man that allowed a bitch to use him. Now get out of my way and stay out of my life."

He was being his old stubborn self as he gazed into my eyes the way he did on our wedding day to say, "I still love you now more than ever."

Hearing him tell me he how he loved me more now than ever angered me. When I needed his love, he didn't give it to me. When I was about to kill myself, I needed to feel his love, and I didn't get it. Now after a year of separation, he wants to love me because he sees a new me and other men wanting me; it pissed me off.

Glaring into his lying eyes, I stated "What's love got to do with it, when you gave your love to another family? You know the one you married in front of God first and now have a son that looks not like you."

His countenance dropped as he moved out my way. I got out feeling like a step had been accomplished in my life towards him. Ahmad continued to stand there. I went in the store, and he was still standing there when I came out. Twisting my neck in a no fashion, verbally my words were, "You gave up the right to act like my husband, or do you not remember that day of our wedding?"

"Ty, things happened. We can't change it, but you must believe me."

"Believe you is like believing a dog with teeth won't bite in the future."

"Ty, you don't get it. You still don't understand. I made a mistake, and I am seeing things differently."

"You can see things all you want; the fact of the matter hasn't changed. I raised our son alone for a year. He cried for you just as hard as I did when we left. I don't think you get it, if anything. We were your family, and you left us out in the cold. You choose a well-known slut over me. So why not become what you wanted."

"Ty, I know this has not been easy for you but please try to understand."

"Understand? What do you want from me? I gave you my everything until I had nothing left to give. I got to the end of my rope and didn't want to live without you, but Josiah is the reason I'm still here. You underestimated the pain, humiliation, and disbelief you caused me. So don't tell me that I don't understand. You only thought about the good dick feeling she was giving you. You didn't think about me and your real son."

"I just want to talk to you."

Deciding I have had enough of listening to him, point blank I stated, "If we aren't talking about Josiah or when we filing for divorce, we don't have anything to talk about."

Ahmad acted like the wind was knocked out of him when he repeated, "You want a divorce?"

Bucking my eyes at him I said, "You tell me why I shouldn't want one?"

He looked down as if to remember. When he got an answer he said, "You don't believe in it and neither do I."

I turned my head from him than back towards him with a response of, "I didn't believe in a lot of things, but you made a believer out of me. Now goodbye, I have a date tonight."

Turning back to unlock my car door, he asked seriously and sternly, "With who?"

Without looking at him I said, "You don't have the right to ask me that, and I won't answer that. You gave up that right the day you stopped being my husband."

"Have you forgotten you're still my wife?"

"Have you forgotten that you live with another

woman that acts like the wife? Looks like someone have taken my place and the impostor has been living my life; don't I feel like sucking eggs?"

"Ty, don't do this. Go back to being you."

"Being me! Being me is what got me without you. And I can't go back to being the old me, no more than we can go back in time and change what you created."

"I never meant to hurt you. I never meant to hurt you."

"A mistake happens once; it does not keep going. If it keeps going, it is no longer a mistake. You know what you are doing and evidently you enjoy what you are doing."

I drove off as my heart calmed down. My car stopped in front of my apartment before my nerves became calmed. I got out the car and low and behold, Bianca was standing out front. Paying her no attention, I began to walk towards my door. She yelled out, "I don't know what you trying to prove by moving over here. Ahmad don't love you or the new you."

My steps halted. Turning to face her, I said "If you have him like you do, then how he does or does not love me shouldn't affect you, since he is legally my husband. And if I want to come in your house and get my husband, you won't and can't stop me."

"You try bringing your ass in here is all I have to

say."

I walked off and called Blackie. He answered and I asked, "How do you feel about me coming over tonight and chilling?"

"That sounds nice. There is nothing like a good conversation."

"When you get off, get changed and come across the parking lot and get me."

"Ahmad and my sister being in the house won't bother you?"

"Does it bother you?"

He gave me a nice chuckled and said, "You are most definitely a woman I can get used to."

"Bye."

I unlocked my door and my cell rung. I spoke, "What's up?"

"You dodging my calls like I took your husband or something."

"J Lamb, no body's dodging you."

"You got time to tell me about you and Blackie; it's been a few since we chat it up?"

"I have a few minutes. We went to the parking lot at Wal-Mart."

"Wal-Mart! His ass that cheap or that broke?"

"I wanted to go there and chill."

"Chilling at Wal-Mart? You must be out your mind."

"No. I asked to sit there and talk."

"Talk?"

"Listen, we talked for a long time, and I like his company. He made me feel comfortable and we have many things in common."

"The only thing y'all have in common is how a brother and sister is in the marriage of a husband and wife."

You can't help but to laugh at J Lamb. I said, "I did a strip tease dance on my break with Ahmad and his friends watching."

"He was furious, wasn't he?"

"He was when he confronted me at Fred's a while ago."

"He what?"

"Yes, he told me I'm not the woman he knows and how I have changed. Get this; he said he still loves me."

"No, he didn't?"

"Yes, I told him, he took his love and gave it to

another family."

"You told him that? What he say?"

"He really looked hurt by what I said. Soon as I made it home, Bianca fronts on me by telling me that I'm wrong if I think Ahmad still love me."

"You tell her he said he did?"

"No. I told her if I want to come in her house and get my husband, I was going to do just that."

J Lamb began to act up like he was there. Next thing, I know he said, "Don't whip her until I get there."

"Boy, I'm not fighting shit. Fuck that. I don't have to fight for something that belongs to me. But I did call Blackie and told him I want to come to his house tonight and chill."

"You a bad bitch. You going in her house?"

"The only thing she can do is shut the fuck up and sit down."

"Look my phone will be off."

"Why haven't you paid your bill?"

"It's either pay my bill or don't eat."

"Which you do?"

"I didn't pay my bill, and I eat at dads anyway."

"What you do with the money?"

"I partied."

I laughed as I hung up on him. Going to my room, I showered and changed into a nice outfit that goes with tennis shoes, in case I have to put them on her face. About an hour later, Blackie came home. Another hour later, he knocked on the door. I opened up and he said, "You sure you going to be ok about being in the house with them?"

"Why wouldn't I be? He made up his mind a year ago."

We walked back across the street. Blackie opened the door, and Ahmad could have sunk through the spot he sat. Bianca came out of the kitchen and said, "Get that bitch out of here."

"Whoa, she, my guest. I pay bills here too. If she wants to come over, she's coming over."

Kindly as ever, I said "Thank you Blackie."

"Wait until your girlfriend, I mean wife finds out."

Putting Ahmad on blast, Blackie said, "Tell her. Ty and I are friends and friends chill, don't they, Ahmad?"

My husband did not look up at Blackie. He kept his eyes fixed on me. Flashing him a winner smile, I tugged on his arm and asked, "Let's go to your room, I'm ready to lie down."

Ahmad got up and stormed out the house. Bianca said, "The game you playing, I've done it. How you think I got your husband?"

"By being a free fuck and an easy target that is why he's still not married to you."

She came at me, but Blackie defended me by saying, "Stay back B. You asked for it, and she gave it to you. Any time she wants to be here with me, she can be. Ty is my company and is here for me. Now we are going in my room. If you don't want her here, leave; Ahmad did."

I humped my shoulders in a childish form as he said, "After you."

"Thank you, Blackie."

We went in his room, and he locked the door. We chuckled as he said, "She mad as hell at me. I know she is going to tell my old girl."

"We just friends. Let her tell her."

Blackie turned the slow jam music down low as he sat on one recliner and I sat on the other one. Believe it or not he was the perfect gentleman. We laughed and I laughed louder than I normal mainly if I heard someone coming by the door. Never had I thought I would be in this house and delighting myself in this man's company.

It was getting close to midnight, and I yawned.

"You ready to go, aren't you?"

186

"Sad, but it's true."

"It's funny how I haven't thought about sex. I like your company too much to mess that up."

"I am glad because I have things going on and I don't need any more stress."

"Ok."

He got my jacket and placed it on me. He opened the door, and I walked out in front of him. Bianca was on the couch sleeping. He opened the front door and said, "Ahmad must not be home because she always sleeps on the couch when he is out."

"I don't want to talk about them at all. How they are or how anything? My husband made his mind up a year ago, and I have respected his wishes. Your sister needs to realize that she is not the wife, and how she has my husband."

"My sister is used to getting her way and any man. For what it is worth, he is not that happy if you ask me."

"I'm not asking, and I don't want to know."

"You right, but I know he doesn't like me with you. I can tell by the way he looks at you. He still loves you."

"You on my side or his?" I said as I placed my hands on my hips.

"Hey, I'm just being honest."

187

"Keep it up."

"I plan to."

He and I began to walk across the parking lot and no Ahmad. I gave him a hug, and he waited until I went in. I closed the door and went in my room. While in the process of getting undressed, Ahmad appeared out of my bathroom. I screamed but calmed down when I saw it was him.

"What are you doing here? How you get in here?"

Tears were down his face as he gave me a lost country boy in the city look. I turned away from him because it reminded me of our wedding, mostly of the vows he said to me. I spoke using as much authority as I could by saying, "Get out. We have nothing to say. In fact, you are trespassing."

My husband ignored my statements and asked, "Did you have sex with him?"

"You asking the wrong question to the wrong one."

"Did you have sex with him? I know how he is, and I know he fakes at being a good guy. He has sex more than the average man. Tell me did you have sex with him?"

"What's it to you if I did or didn't? You have been having sex far longer than I have so why you want to know what I am or am not doing? My name is Tygeria, not Bianca. I supposed to be the wife, not the outside woman. Our roles are messed up. It is clear what you need to ask is, who is the real father of that baby you take care of and why our son doesn't have his father in his life? Plus whom I give it up to, is irrelevant."

Ahmad began to break down like he did when he found out his mom passed. He was irrational and hysterical as tears soaked his shirt. I didn't know what to do because at first, I thought he was playacting, but this is the real thing. He sat on my bed and stated as soon as his voice was able to, "Please tell me. I have been the only man you ever slept with, and I just need to know if someone else has had you, Ty."

"You want to know if his is better than yours or if any other man I may have had better than yours? That is what you really want to know, don't you? You really want to know if I still crave for sex I don't get with you."

I was unprepared for Ahmad's anger as he snatched me off my feet and threw me on the bed. I began to fight back but he ousted me in upper body strength. The next thing I knew, he had my own gun pointed to my head. This has never been seen before. I was scared senseless. The fear in his eyes told me that he was being tortured by his actions, but that is on him to handle his own demons. He made choices like I did and either way we must acknowledge them, good or bad.

For the life of me, I don't get it how or why he is so angry about me and other men, whereas, he has been living with a woman for over a year. He was shaking as he said, "Ty, please baby please, don't make me kill you. I love you. I never stopped loving you, and I can't take it. I swear I can't take it. I thought I could, but I can't take it. The shit is real and no more games. No man needs to know about you, fat or not. You are my wife! MY WIFE! Did you have sex with him and don't lie because I know when you lie. God, I know when you lie."

Tears were down my face as I am now faced with the reality of my feelings.

"No. I have friends, but I haven't had sex since you. You satisfied, now? No man has touched me because I still loved you. I am a woman, and I want to be wanted by a man that wants me for me, but I have to get over you. Just in case you don't get it, this marriage has been over since that day at the church."

He fell over sobbing into my comforter set. Parts of me wanted to comfort him, but I couldn't. I didn't want to play the wife part and not be the wife. So many emotions went through me as I listened to him. Ahmad is hurting, but so was I.

Turning my head, I continued to listen to him say something to God. This is the first time I had heard him cry this long and hard. Not just that but he is crying out to the Lord, I think as he lay on my bed sobbing. This entire night has been mind-blowing as I continued to lie in the spot afraid to move.

His present state is unknown to me and making any sharp moves could distract him and make him hurt me.

Ahmad has never been violent towards me and has never shown this side of himself. Then it hit me, I am winning the strike against Ahmad, but at what price?

CHAPTER 10

Somewhere along the way, I woke up an hour earlier with the thought that he was still there. I was alone, and Ahmad was gone. For half an hour, I sat there on the bed confused. I got my phone; I called Pastor Tatum. If my memory serves me right, he is always up because he works for the city of Louisville, so he is up praying or watching the news.

He answered the phone in his normal tone, "Good morning."

I started to hang up but didn't. I responded, "Good morning."

"Tygeria, is this you?"

"Yes, Sir, it is."

"Is everything ok?"

"It is and it isn't."

"Go on."

"Ahmad broke into my place and put a gun to my head. He was crying and saying that he still loves me and stuff. I haven't seen him like that in a long time, and it scared me."

He was quiet for a second before saying, "My son is realizing that he messed up, so this means you are seeing someone, and he doesn't approve of it."

"I am not dating, but I do have friends. One of the guys is his little girlfriend's brother."

"That explains it. To me he didn't realize just how it would be to see you with another man until he has actually seen you with another man. Now that he has, it makes him angry, and he doesn't know why."

"Why should it matter, he has been involved with another woman before we got married and he is still with her? Not just that she claims it is his son, but he doesn't look like him to me."

"I had been talking to my son ever since you been gone. He loves you and you are still his wife."

"Pastor, what good is being his wife when he has never made me feel like a wife? Do you not remember soon as we were pronounced husband and wife, Bianca was there and has not left? When did I have time to be a wife to him?"

"Tygeria, you haven't and believe me he is resenting his actions of deserting you and Josiah more than you know."

"If he resents it like that, why is he still with her? Why he never comes after his son and me to make things right?"

"Some things can't be explained and for him to

come into your place and cry, that should tell you something."

"It tells me to get my divorce and stay away from him."

"I hope divorce is not the option you both choose."

"You mean I choose. He chose it on our wedding day; I just been dragging my feet."

"Come by today and bring Josiah."

"I won't get him until Friday. I have to find a sitter before he can stay here in Louisville with me."

"You in Louisville? I thought you were back here in Ackerman?"

"I didn't want to live in Ackerman anymore. I actually live in the same housing complex where he lives but across the parking lot."

"Ty, you playing with danger."

"Pastor, everyone only sees what I am doing. No one pays attention to what he has done to me and my son. You all say how I have to be tread lightly but what about him? Where is the accountability Ahmad has to pay? No one says to him how living with another woman and being married is wrong. I haven't heard anyone say how she taunted me on my wedding day and was out of line. Soon as I say where I live, I am in the wrong."

"I didn't say it was your fault."

"Funny Sir that is all I hear when I listen to you, and my brother talk. I have a life but according to you both, I can't live it because I am married. You know more than anyone how devastated I was over your son. Now I have lost weight, and my confidence level is higher, I'm the evil one."

The phone line was quiet.

"Tygeria, I still believe you, and Ahmad can make this work. I still believe in the power of prayer and the move of God."

"Huh, I gave up making it work the day I left Mississippi and when he didn't come after me."

The line was quiet again.

"There is a reason why this has happened to you. Sooner or later, you will have to face the fact, whatever it may be."

Cutting him off, I spoke, "I didn't get married by myself, but I will chat later. I have to get ready for work. By the way, I work in the office at Taylor's."

I hung up because I know he will have something to say about that. Taking a shower, I put on another dress but with knee high boots. This time, I allowed my bouncy hair to hang to the top of my shoulders. Just the way Ahmad loves it. While staring into the mirror, I saw a woman that still wants the approval of her husband.

This woman is still in love with him but wants to move on. Honestly, I thought that removing myself from his life would help me with mine. Most of it is because I desired to be the type of woman he fell for and so far, it has worked. Taking a sigh, I put on a smile and headed out to work. On my way, I called and checked on Josiah.

As usual, he was doing well and up with my brother. Josh loves being the role model for Josiah and I am glad. My brother is the type of guy I want my son to take after. I used to want him to be like his father because he looks like him, but his dad's actions are not those my son needs to imitate. The parking lot was getting full as I pulled in front of the building.

Thank God, I don't have to park across the street like others. I spoke to all those in my path as I watched for Ahmad. Hours passed by and I kept looking for him. I saw the list and noticed that he called in sick. Sick? I thought as I played it off and continued to do my work. On my break, I went to the Cash Savers deli.

I walked in, not to order, but to be seen. I wasn't hungry but picked up a side order of peach pie. Some of his friends were there, and they were watching me. Like a hoe in distress, I smiled and walked off with a little more ump in my step. Before I reached my car, his fine slow friend Devin came over and offered to open the door.

Placing the order on top of the car, I stood in the door

and said thoughtfully, "Why thank you, Devin."

"You remembered me?"

"How can I forget? We met at the club when I came into town. Remember how you scanned my body?"

He began to blush. I gave him a sexual look down as I smiled and asked, "What? You still standing at my door like I owe you a tip."

He smiled as he said, "I want to ask you something?"

"Open your mouth and ask."

He smiled and asked, "Can I take you out?"

"I don't know, can you?"

"May I take you out?"

"Maybe who knows. Your girlfriend slash fiancé approached me the other day."

"She told me."

"I don't feel comfortable placing myself in the presence of a man that allows other women to front the woman he wants to see."

He was quiet as he stated, "That won't happen again."

"I know it won't because if it does, I will give her something to front me about."

"Let me get a grip on that."

Shaking my head I spoke, "I don't know. Women like me need a man to have his things in order and not put them in order on an as-need basis."

"How do I know there won't be any problems on your end with Ahmad?"

I closed the door. I got close to him and indicated, "You should be worried about what I have to say, not him."

He looked down at me and spoke, "I'm not worried, but I don't want a man to front on me about being in your face."

"Then why you in my face, if I'm not what you want?"

"You have a pretty face."

"Does it matter? I mean really matter if I have a husband I have not been with for over a year?"

"No."

"Then quit asking questions if it makes no difference."

I opened the door and got in my vehicle. He was still there. I allowed a little thigh to be seen and like a man, he looked and smiled. I tugged at the dress to lower it. Cranking up I left him watching. Before I parked, I got a phone call. Orally, I said "I haven't heard from this nigga in a while."

It was Tony from Utah. I wonder if his wife is enjoying the fact that I've left. Luckily, she only ran her mouth on the phone. If she had caused me grief, than keeping her man would not be a problem. I began to laugh silently because Tony always makes me laugh and if hadn't, I would have canned his ass a long time ago.

"Hello."

"You sound sexy this afternoon."

"I always sound sexy. What's going on?"

"I miss you."

"Sure, you do. You at home with your wife and daughter, you should be happy."

"But you not here and that don't make me happy. When am I going to see you?"

"When you have more money to spend on me? I am tired of you taking me to the same old places, doing the same old things."

"I kept your hair fixed, nails done, bills paid and fancy attire. I'm doing my part to keep you satisfied."

"In case, you forgot, I bore easily."

"Bay, chill, just relax. I have vacation time coming up. I can take you to the mountains for a few days or we can go to Hawaii like you wanted. Better yet, I can come where you at."

"You don't need to come here, and I don't need you here. You need to stay with your wife and keep her out my hair because she called me the day I left. If I had stayed, you'll be with me."

"Tell me where you at?"

"No. I'm not your wife, and I have loose ends to tie up here."

"You can be."

"Well, not this time. If you aren't talking about spending any money on me, you need to get off my line."

"Spending money on you is not a problem."

"I hear you running your mouth and not running your hand in your wallet."

He gave me a gracious laugh as he spoke, "You are so assertive and that is what I admire most about you."

"Pay me just right, and I can teach your wife how to keep you at home."

He laughed again as he said, "You can tell her all you want. She is no longer what I want."

"Well, I have to go. State your claim."

"I want to see you and be with you. I have some

money to spend on you."

"You said some, and I am not a some type of woman."

"How much you need me to send to you?"

"None, because you will know what state I'm in, and I don't need you trying to complicate what I have going here."

"You have another nigga?"

"I don't just have a nigga; I have a husband."

He laughed as I said, "I will call you back later. You can pay my phone bill for another three months. If you can't do anything for me, stay off my line. Verizon's plans and data is not cheap, and I am not a cheap bitch."

"Consider phone bill paid."

"Good, so call me later."

"Ok."

I got out the car and went back in to work. An hour later I got a text saying my phone bill has been paid four hundred dollars in advance. I smiled and text Tony: You did your part, and when I get back, I will do my part.

He replied, "Can't wait."

The rest of the day went off with a hitch. It went by fast. I had to call J Lamb but forgot his phone off. I didn't want to go to Ackerman, so I paid my best friend's phone bill. It wasn't but fifty-five dollars. "Such small amount" I thought as paid it. Soon as I clocked out and got on Highway Fifteen, J Lamb called me.

"I must be some kind of popular because my bill got paid, and I know you did it."

"I didn't feel like driving to Ackerman to talk to you that's why paid it, but once I paid it I forgot I told your dad I would come by."

"You need to feel like that more often."

"Doubt it."

"What's good?"

"Let's see, I chilled with Blackie in his apartment."

Yelling loudly, "You have to tell me all about it!"

Responding just as confident, "What you want to know?"

"What my brother say?"

"After he stared me down, he said nothing but left out."

"What she say?"

"She tried throwing a fit and telling Blackie that she doesn't want me there, but he told her that she can't do that because he pays bills. Also, is she don't like it she could leave out like Ahmad did."

"I would have loved to have seen her face."

"He even told her that anytime I wanted to come over and chill with him I could. Then she threatened him by saying his old girl will know. He told her it was ok because he and I are just friends."

"What she say?"

"Nothing. We went in the room and listened to music as we talked."

"No sex?"

"None."

"You lying?"

"Seriously, no sex. We have a lot in common though, and we enjoy talking to each other."

"No sex, for real?"

"Yes, for real."

"Is he gay?"

"He doesn't act like it to me."

"I'm just saying. You been dressed like a hoe for the times you been with him, and he hasn't made a move on you. The brother is gay."

I laughed as I said, "That's not the best half."

"What is?"

"Your brother broke into my place."

"He what?"

"Broke into my place and kept asking me if sex with Blackie has occurred?"

"You told him no."

"I did but he kept being persistent and not believing me. When he realized that I was telling the truth, it is when he had thrown me on the bed and put a gun to my head."

"You done made my quiet brother snap!"

"I did not."

"You lying! Ain't no way he gone put a gun to your head if he wasn't still in love with you."

"I don't know about all that, but he did. When he saw I was really telling the truth, he starts crying and I was so scared, I did not move. The next thing, I know it was almost time for me to get up for work."

"You call daddy?"

"I did, but he did not believe me."

"Why you say that?"

"I told him he is like my brother, they only care about how Ahmad is but when I mention where I live or this and that I am wrong in some form. They only think I am doing this out of spite."

"Are you?"

"At first, I thought about that, but I have to live my life. I have a son, and we need some type of closure."

"What's next now?"

"Divorce."

"You trying to get my brother to do a murder suicide?"

"No, he has a life, why can't I?"

"You can, just not in Mississippi."

"You know I am beginning to believe that."

"What you got planned today?"

"Don't know; what you got up?"

"No gas to go anywhere."

"J Lamb, you need to manage your money better."

"I know but time is hard when there is pussy to buy and a life style to maintain."

"Stop it."

"Sounds good, don't it?"

"I know right."

"Come on over and fuck with me, tonight."

"I'll come."

"You can follow me. I'm on my way to go see your dad."

"You know what, I'll meet you at your place; I don't need a sermon."

Laughing I got off the phone with him and turned into Pastor Tatum's home. Before I came to a complete stop, my phone rung and I did not know the number. Going against my conscious, I answered it "Hello."

"Is this Tygeria?"

"This is she."

"This is a friendly reminder for you to stop seeing Blackie."

A grin came into play as I spoke, "I can see with my two eyes who I want. If you don't want him seeing me, tell him not to see me."

"I already heard about you."

"I promise what you heard is nothing like I will show you, if you keep playing on my phone."

206

"I am not playing; he is mine and you can't have him."

"If he is yours, why you calling me about someone that belongs to you?"

"Oh, you a smart ass. I heard that, too."

"Hear what you want, I have an agenda, and you are not on it. I advise you to take whatever problem you have up with him and leave me out of it. I can't and won't do anything that he doesn't want me to do."

"Consider this a warning to stay away from my man."

"Consider this a warning, if you acting like this and I haven't slept with him yet; imagine what you going to do when I give it to him."

She began yelling into the phone. For the most of her words, I could not understand it but when she said, "When I see that ass, I'm getting it" I heard it.

Being me, I replied "When you see this ass bring some ass because I'm getting it."

I hung up and quickly called Blackie. He answered by saying, "Tiger Stripes, what gives the pleasure today?"

"I haven't slept with you, but your girlfriend/wife or whoever she is, is calling me."

"She what?"

"Called me telling me she going to beat my ass for being your friend."

"Don't worry about that. Let me call you back."

I knew he was calling her, and I know it's going to work out to my advantage because in today's time, bitches are over wives and other women especially if the man loves to flirt and possibly wants to sleep with you. About ten minutes later, I was about to get out when my phone rung. I answered it. "Hello."

"Someone has something to say to you."

"I'm sorry I stepped out of line. I was wrong to contact you."

It was Blackie's woman. She sounded like she had been crying, but I didn't care. She has no business contacting me and fronting me over dick I am not getting.

"Next time stay in your place."

The next voice I heard on the phone was Blackie's as he said, "I'm sorry about that."

"It's good. We just friends and that's all."

"She needs to save that for the women you really may be sleeping with."

He laughed as he said, "Now I have to go in here and get on her ass some more for doing that childish shit. Either she has me, or she doesn't."

"It seems like she isn't sure she has you."

"She knows I am feeling someone, and she's on her way out the door."

"You better get on her for doing that because the next woman may not be as nice as I was."

We laughed a few more minutes. I saw Pastor Tatum come outside. I spoke, "I am at the preacher's house. I'll hit you back up later if I get a chance to."

"It doesn't matter I know when you at home."

I laughed and hung up. I smiled and finally noticed that there was a new car there, but other than that the place still had its touch. Many days I ate over here with Ahmad's family. The cook outs, the dinners and holidays were mostly spent here. Whenever Josh was busy working to take care of me, Ahmad's family took me in.

They made me feel love and that brought me out of the depression condition I had been in. J Lamb introduced me to his brother and together they introduced me to their parents. I was a regular and quite naturally I fell in love with Ahmad and him me. Just recalling my life here and how I had loved him made my eyes water up, but I couldn't let them fall.

I got out the car and began walking towards the back patio like always. I took my phone out and placed it on silent. Pastor Tatum said, "Tygeria, you look lovely."

He is the only man that could say a compliment, and it isn't taken out of context to me. Other than Josh, Pastor Tatum became my dad when I didn't have one. When I was wrong, he and his wife told me. For being with them I can't forget, and I can't repay them for all they had done for me and my brother.

Walking up the steps, I gave Pastor a hug. He gave me that famous smile of his that usually tells me that everything is going to be alright.

"Before we go in, I need you to know there is a reason, I asked you to come over. Don't be angry but allow me to do this for you."

He went in first and when I came in behind him, I saw Ahmad. My heart was fluttering as the sight of him filled my eyes. I dared not to speak but the look on my face told them that I was not pleased one bit.

"Sit down, Tygeria."

I still did not say a word. Shortly after I sat down, my phone lit up. I spoke, "Excuse me."

It was Tony, and I wasn't going to answer it but figured why not. "Hello."

"Babe what you doing?"

I tried to turn my phone off speaker, which I did on purpose so Ahmad could hear another man's voice. He jumped up screaming, "Who is he?"

"He's my business and not yours."

Tony was on the other end yelling, "Tell that punk who I am!"

"Goodbye Tony. I'll call you later."

When I hung up, Ahmad was staring as he said, "He been around my boy?"

"Don't come questioning me about who's been in his life! All you need to know is that you haven't been in his life."

"Is that your man!"

Pastor Tatum got up and got between us. Now this is the second time, in less than a day that Ahmad has acted some type of way. I could only stare at him as he said, "I don't like a lot of men coming around Josiah."

"Are you around Josiah?"

Ahmad turned around and yelled, "Ooh you make me so mad, with games you play."

"I'm playing games! Try this game, let's get a divorce."

They both stopped and stared at me as if I cursed in a church. Ahmad fell back into his seat with a blank look on his face.

"Tygeria, are you sure you want to do that?"

"Pastor there was a time in my life when I wasn't sure but after waiting for him for over a year, I think it's wrong of you to ask me if I am sure."

"A divorce," Ahmad spoke above a whisper.

"You act like this was not coming. You have never been a husband to me, legally. You been practicing on a woman, excuse me Pastor, that only has good sex and head. You never wanted to be real with me because you the one that had been playing."

"But a divorce?"

"This is not brand new to you."

"Do you love me?"

I walked over to the window and looked out as he asked again, "Do you not still love me?"

"Ahmad my feelings for you were never in question you gave away your family for another one. So don't ask me about if I love you or not because I have loved you forever, but now after seeing you being so happy, I must let you go so you can make her your wife. To be frank with you, I left so I could stop loving you."

"You both need to wait for three more months."

"Pastor I've been waiting a year for him, so I guess waiting three more months to be free of him won't hurt."

I sat down opposite from him, but Pastor asked me

to move on the same couch. It didn't have to be side by side but on the same couch. Politely, I asked, "This morning when I called, you knew what happened already, didn't you?"

"Yes. Ahmad came over to the house and told me all about it."

"Then, why am I here?"

"He didn't go to work today because he has been here clearing his mind."

I still did not say a word. I noticed that Ahmad was not looking at me either. I asked, "What is the point of me being here for him to clear his mind?"

"Ahmad," Pastor said as he looked at his son to speak.

I turned sideways, slightly to listen to him. He said, "My actions have not been that of a man but, Tygeria, I have never stopped loving you."

I stood up and said, "Wait, I've heard this before. I don't need you to go out in the world and do what you want then expect me to run to you with open arms. It's just not going to happen. Save those vows for the woman you really love."

"Tygeria, sit down and listen to him" Pastor spoke to urge me to hear his son out.

"Listen to him! That is all I have ever done and look

how it got me, broken hearted, lonely and now self-made."

"I told you she won't listen" Ahmad said to his dad as I glared back at him.

"You only want to talk to me because I have lost a lot of weight, and I look good."

"That's not true. Your weight has never been a problem for me. I love you for you."

"So those things she said to me in front of you were not true."

"I said those things just to make you look bad. I didn't know she would tell you. I got caught up, and now I am seeing the error of my ways."

"Stupid, how could you not think she would not take the opportunity to tell me what you say about me? Women do devious things just for a man. I should know; I've had my share."

"Tygeria, I wanted you here so you both can discuss Josiah."

"What about my son?"

"He's my son, too."

"Your son starved to death and doesn't remember who you are."

Ahmad gave me a dumb look as I said that to him. He

214

then said, "You lying because my son remembers me. I was there for him when he was two."

"Why does everyone call me a liar? I have no reason to lie. Ask J Lamb? When he came to pick us up, Josiah said daddy. I said no, that's Uncle Jamal. When we saw my brother, he remembered somewhat but when he started being with him, he remembered my brother. Now you, the absent father, you might have a problem because I never mentioned your name around him because when we first left, he cried for you just as much as I did. You remember me telling you that?"

He shook his head, yes. "I was not lying. He grieved you and I vowed not to have him hurt again by someone that didn't want to be there for him. Now you not wanting me is one thing but to totally exclude yourself from him for a year was all you."

"I want to make that up to him, and I don't want every ball and dick around him."

"I don't do that but if I wanted to I could. It sounds to me that you mad because you're not a part of every ball and dick around him. Truth be told, you just a face in the crowd when it comes to my son knowing who you are. But as much as I want to have you disappear, I wouldn't do that to Josiah. Honestly, he needs you just as much but when a man finds me worthy, Josiah will have a real father there for him."

"Come on you two. You are here to discuss Josiah

not your personal feelings towards one another."

Ahmad's tone changed as he said, "Tygeria, I will make it up to him, and you, too, if you let me."

"What about your other son, you know the one that lives in the house with you?"

"I plan to blood test him."

"Planning? I've seen the way you plan. Never mind, that is not my concern."

"You always make this about you."

"I suppose to be the acting wife. It's always going to be about me, how I think and for sure how I feel."

He must have realized that I wasn't backing down, so he did what he does best, changed the topic. "Where is Josiah?

"I didn't have a sitter for him, so Josh and Jessica were keeping him for me. I get him tomorrow."

"Tygeria, could you go get him?" Pastor Tatum asked.

"For you, I will."

I left out and J Lamb was parked a little way by the barn as I was leaving out. I rolled down he window and he said, "You bout to go?"

"I knew you were there somewhere lurking

around."

"And miss drama, a lie."

We did a short-lived laugh as he asked, "So you fixing to go?"

"No, Ahmad wants to see Josiah."

"Tell Ahmad he can play daddy toma. I'm ready to get to Louisville today. I'm just glad you came on. I was getting tired of waiting on you."

Realizing he is up to something, I asked "Who you going to see?"

"I'm going to see a man about a dog."

"You hate dogs."

"Next answer, I'm going to see this woman, so I can sell her my land in Florida."

"You don't have land in Florida."

"That means you don't need to know who I'm going to go see."

From the faint light, I saw that he was indeed inpatient. I asked, "What you got to do in Louisville that you need me to do in a hurry?"

"I don't need you."

"Then go on to Louisville without me."

"See you playing games now."

"You said you didn't need me."

"Bout like a Negro. You know I don't have gas money."

"Right, so you need me?"

"Yeah, I need you to give me ten dollars."

"Here's ten dollars for you."

As I handed him the money, I took my house key off and said, "Here, I will be on sooner or later. Your brother wants to be daddy this evening."

"He might as well be daddy this evening; the one in that house, isn't nowhere near his."

"That's him. Let me go get Josiah. See you in a few."

CHAPTER 11

I drove off and headed to Josh's house. I turned into his driveway and got out. I saw Jessica looking out the window. She saw that it was me; she opened the door. "Hey there, is everything alright?"

"Yeah, I come to get Josiah earlier."

"Ok, but I am sure Josh won't like it."

"Where he at?"

"He still at work."

"Where Josiah?"

"He is in the family room watching TV."

My son ran to me when he saw me. I kneeled down and gave him a mighty squeeze.

"Get your things mommy has a surprise for you."

"Surprise for me?"

"Yes, a surprise for you so come on."

I stood up and said, "I was at Pastor Tatum's, and Ahmad was there."

"You and him in the same room? What gives?"

"I think he wants to start over, but I am unclear of his plans. I've already been hurt by him, and do not want it to happen again."

"What does this have to do with Josiah?"

"He wants to see him and start making things up to him and me."

"Ty, it sounds like he wants to get his proper family back. Pray about it first so this can't be a ploy of some type."

"Jessica, he can want all he wants. God himself will have to tell me to take him back. Do you not know all I had been through with him?"

"I'm a woman and you know I know, but we don't know what God has in store for us. Look at your brother and me. I've been with Josh since I was in the fifth grade, and it took well over twenty years for us to have one child. We might have wanted to be ready, but it wasn't God's time, so guess what? It wasn't our time. So, you never know how he may come telling you about Ahmad. Don't knock the thought completely out, just yet."

"You right but why do they all think that it's all on me and none of it is on him?"

"Worldly, that is just how men think. It's like Ahmad wanted you to wait until he made up his mind to have you and Josiah and by that he thought you would have remained single, right?"

"Yeah, but I have been single. I mean I have friends

but that is about all it is. I haven't been sexually involved with anyone. Maybe that is my problem. Maybe I need to jump into bed like he did."

"I won't advise you to do that, either. Just be patient and keep on doing what you been doing because evidently, it's been working and now you have his attention, keep it."

"You right. Thanks, Jessica."

Josiah came downstairs, and I asked Jessica, "Where Te-Te baby?"

"She is asleep. I had her getting her shots today. I pumped her full of Tylenol for children, and she is out."

Smiling I said, "I remember those days."

She walked us to the door, and we waved by to her. I locked Josiah down and headed back to Pastor Tatum's farm. We pulled up and I said, "Mommy wants you to visit your grandpa."

"My grandpa?"

"Grandpa Tatum."

"Grandpa Tatum."

When the Range Rover came to a complete stop, Josiah unbuckled himself. I opened the door for him. Holding his hand, we went up the steps, and Pastor Tatum opened the door. He saw Josiah, and he was completely covered with joy as always when he is seeing his only grandchild, thus far. I could see the baffled look on Ahmad's face as our son fled from him. I spoke, "Josiah, don't you want to see daddy?"

He shook his head, yes. Grabbing him by his small hand, I walked him a few feet to his father and Josiah said, "Daddy?"

"Daddy's here."

Josiah screamed out, "Daddy!"

This time, he reached for Ahmad and held him so tight. I wanted to cry because my son had wanted his father for over a year and now, he has his father, it touched my heart. Pastor looked at me with an approval look and left the room. Ahmad sat back down and put Josiah in his lap.

Josiah asked, "You gone leave us?"

Ahmad looked up at me and I shook my head, no. He replied, "Little man, I am not leaving you ever again. I love you so much. You hear me?"

"Yes."

Josiah looked at Ahmad and asked, "What about mommy?"

"Mommy is loved, too."

Each time, he said daddy I could feel the love Ahmad had every time he heard his son call him daddy. I sat on the other end of the couch and listened to Josiah talk and talk

Ahmad's ears off. I hadn't heard my son talk so much in my life, but here he is chatting away with his daddy.

I could not resist as I took a picture of them side by side. When I showed them the picture, Josiah said "Daddy, you look like me."

That was too funny as Ahmad replied, "I do look like you, and you are very handsome."

"Mommy, we handsome?"

"Yes, you are."

"Send it to my phone" Ahmad asked out the blue.

"I don't have your number."

He took out his phone and called me. J Lamb was right; he still had my number. I saved his number under Baby Daddy and sent him the picture. He got the picture and made it his home screen. Josiah was having so much fun, but I was tired.

"Josiah, honey, it's time for us to go."

"No, mommy, I want to play with daddy."

"You can see him later. I have to go to work, and your daddy has to go home."

"Can we go home with daddy?"

"No, your daddy has too many people at his house, isn't that right daddy?"

He looked sad as he said dryly, "Yeah."

Josiah began to cry as I was trying to take him from Ahmad. He didn't want Josiah to go just as much as Josiah didn't want to go. Pastor Tatum came out and said, "How about if Josiah stays the night here with me and tomorrow when Ahmad gets off, he can bring him to you?"

"Please mommy can I stay with grandpa and daddy?"

"Yes, you can stay. Come give mommy a hug so daddy can walk me outside to get your things?"

Josiah and I hugged. Ahmad opened the door for me. We walked out and I stopped to say, "My son loves you, and I won't see him get hurt."

"Ty, I have my son in my life, and I promise I won't jeopardize it. You don't know how much it means to have him here. There is so much I want to teach him, so much I want to show him."

"Have you forgotten, you have a home with a son?"

"Ty, I plan to move out and come back home. I have to get myself together. What I did last night to you was wrong. What if I had shot you?"

"I don't know."

"I would have robbed my son from you, and I know you love him just as much as he loves you, for that I am sorry. I was overcome with jealousy and still the thought of you with another man makes me delirious. Never mind. But I am going to make it up to you and him. Just give me a chance."

I opened the back door of the car and handed him Josiah's suitcase bag. He reached for it and kept his eyes on me. Bypassing the odd moment, I began to get in as I replied, "I don't know, Ahmad. What I do know is that time heals all wounds. In order for a wound to heal, it can't continue to be opened every chance."

He was still standing as I was sitting in the driver seat. He knocked on the window, and I let the window down. Ahmad said, "You are still beautiful inside and out; even though you have a rough neck attitude that I caused. I want you to know that you always made me happy. You let me see my son and for that I thank you."

Ahmad was bad about putting things on my mind and this was no exception. He made me look at the fact that we were happy at one point. The way my son shined as he saw his dad was wonderful. I had never seen him look like that, and I do everything for him. I know I can't be his father, but I was trying to take that place.

To me I was doing it all, and he was doing nothing. It is true it kind of hurt me to see him that excited about a man that did nothing for him but broke up the family home. But I am human, and I assumed that if I was there for him and he did not want for anything, he would in some form not want to see Ahmad, but that was a mistake I was making.

That was why I didn't keep him from his father because in the later part, he would blame me if I kept his father away. On the other hand, if his father stayed away on his own then I would look like the good guy to my son.

I had no idea that I had made it to my apartment. I was too busy driving and thinking about my personal motives that I became engrossed in making Ahmad feel the emptiness he exemplified towards me. It never really occurred to me the psychological damaged; I could be doing to my son.

Here I am running around playing games with different men and checking women about their husbands and still lonely. The only difference is I haven't been in bed with them because I could not bring myself to sleep with any man. How I long for a man to touch me and make me feel alive, but I was taught better than that.

J Lamb came out my place and spoke, "I was trying to see what was going on?"

Getting out the vehicle I asked, "What was going on?"

"It was taking you too long to come here, and I didn't know if I had time to rummage through your things or not."

Laughing I said, "I was gone longer than I thought."

J Lamb put his arm through mine. We began walking towards my place. He spoke barely above a whisper, "Don't look."

But I turned my head anyway.

"Didn't I say don't look."

"You know you tell people not to look; we look anyway."

"Blackie sitting outside and he have been there all day."

"What?"

"Hurry up, he coming this way."

Before we could enter my door, he called out, "Tiger."

We stopped walking, began turning our heads to search for the voice, as if we didn't know. When I saw him, I spoke, "Oh, hi, there. How you doing?"

"I'm good. Can we talk?"

I looked at J Lamb and said, "Go on. I'll be in in a minute."

"Hello to you, too, Blackie?"

"Sorry about that; hello, Jamal, how are you doing this evening?"

"I'm better."

J Lamb went in the house, and he said, "I want to personally apologize for ole girl calling you about stuff she doesn't know about."

"It's ok but if you were in a relationship, you need to tie up that loose end because it could spell trouble for your future."

"You right, you right. We used to be married, but we are legally separated, and sometimes she gets the two confused."

A car was pulling into the parking lot and with a blink of an eye, Blackie kissed me. I was frozen. Here I am being kissed in a place where my husband could see. When the car parked, Blackie let me go. I looked over and it was Ahmad. He was standing and staring at us.

I screamed out, "Ahmad," but he turned and walked away.

His facial expression was one of disappointment and sadness. Turning back to look at Blackie, he looked at me, and I pushed him back.

"Why you do that for?" I questioned with a surprise.

"That husband of yours needed to know that you are gone on and over him."

"What does that have to do with you kissing me?"

"I wanted to kiss you and anticipated why not now."

"You set that up for him to see you kissing me?"

"He's with my sister fucking her on a daily basis. So, what if I knew he was coming? He needs to see your lips on another man."

I went blank. I knew he was having sex but to know from an insider that it is really real caused my heart to ache. Blackie sensed the wave of sorrow that came over me as he spoke, "Don't tell me you didn't think he was getting it?"

"I don't know what I thought."

"Believe me he's getting it, and he's in love with her."

This could not be as I began to think back earlier when I saw him. Ahmad did not give me any impression that he was in love with Bianca. Then again, I had no clue he was ever cheating on me until that day. Politely I said, "I have to go in, but I may call you earlier, if you know what I mean."

"You mean I get to see those Tiger stripes."

"Yeah, why not, every cat needs to purr."

He smiled, and I gave him a hug. We went back across the street, and I went in the house.

When I locked the door, J Lamb asked quickly, "What the hell was that about? You kissing him at the exact time, Ahmad come back?"

I sat down and said, "J Lamb, something is not right."

"What's not right is that you kissing, Blackie in front of Ahmad. You kissing Blackie period is not right, forget about Ahmad."

"That's just it. You know I just left Ahmad at your dad's."

"Right."

"When I saw him, he didn't act like he is in love with Bianca, but Blackie says he is."

"My brother doesn't love her. He just caught up in the free stuff she does. I'll be caught up, too, if I were him."

"J Lamb, he and I talked and him loving her never came out his mouth. On top of that, Blackie says they have sex on a daily basis."

"I don't know about that."

"Blackie is into some foul shit, and I'm angry about it. To him, he says Ahmad needs to see my lips on another man."

"He up to something, Ty."

"I know, but what?"

About ten minutes passed, and J Lamb said, "Oh I forgot to tell you that Ahmad comes by the house almost every day to see daddy."

"How long he been doing that?"

"Off and on since you been gone."

"How you forget to tell me that?"

"Every time it crossed my mind to tell you, you say you don't want to hear anything about the A word, so I forgot."

"Why he over there for?"

"Girl, he been getting counseling. I think he wants his real family back."

I pulled off my heels and asked, "Back to the subject, what does that have to do with Blackie kissing me?"

"You mean you weren't kissing him?"

"No! He has kissed me somewhat like that, but Ahmad has not ever seen a man kiss me but him, and if I didn't think he planned it, I might could have enjoyed it."

"You mean yo ass been blowing smoke to these niggas, and they doing all this shit because you spit game to them?"

"Yeah."

"Weak bitches!"

I laughed and said, "Forget that. What does he kissing me have to do with anything?"

"Why did he say he kissed you?"

"I told you, he said Ahmad needs to know that I have moved on and see my lips on another man."

J Lamb jumped up and yelled, "That's it! The Black rat playing games."

"How is that when his separated wife slash ole girl whoever she is fronted on me about him, then she called back and apologized."

"I'm telling you, Ty, I smell a black rat."

"You think so?"

"Girl, this is a game, Louisville style."

"You ain't from Louisville."

"Yeah, but I been in the game long enough."

"Explain?"

"He and his sister are in cahoots. She keeps Ahmad from you, and Blackie keeps you from him. They know y'all still love each other."

"Yeah, but I don't feel like that towards Blackie. I have thought about sleeping with him, but that was just a thought."

"He knows that, but I want to say he is doing this for his sister, you know for the family."

"That's logic."

"He does her a favor and in return he gets you."

Sitting back on the soft couch I began to think of what

J Lamb was telling me. It all makes sense, but I was having problems putting it all together. Suddenly my cell rung and I didn't answer.

"Who was that?"

"This man's wife."

"Why she calling you, you ain't got her husband?"

"I know I don't but she for some reason thinks I do."

"They calling you so this must be call a bitch night."

It rung again.

"Put it on speaker, like you did Tony at daddy's house in front of Ahmad tonight."

I laughed as I stated, "Hello."

"Tygeria, this is Tony's wife, Sister Barbara."

"Why are you calling me?"

"My husband is not here, and I assumed he is spending more time with you."

"Barbara, let me tell you like it is before the new me comes out. I don't want your husband. I never had your husband sexually. He was only a friend because he needed someone to talk to. Now if I wanted him dick and all, I could have had it. Since you are calling me, and I am

233

thousands of miles away with no intentions of returning; that means he has finally found someone that is getting more than money. My recommendation to you is pull up your skirt and get out your panties. Your husband is now fucking someone, and it's not me. Now I would appreciate it if you stay off my line and get on his."

I hung up without giving her a chance to respond. Women don't realize that bitches were once good women, too, until a bitch got in her business. Because of said actions, a new attitude and a new of thinking emerges. J Lamb threw a pillow at me to break my thoughts as he said, "Damn, hoes checking you like that? You must be a bad bitch?"

"No, I spend time with lonely men. I give them communication, and they help me out. It's not about sex with me, but I am more confident and wiser than I was a year ago."

"Wish someone will help me out. Truth be told, yo ass still in love with my brother."

"Ahmad's my love, J Lamb. He has been the only man I have loved."

"I think you would take him back if he changed."

J Lamb cell rung and he said, "They say speak of the devil and the devil will appear."

"Ahmad?"

"Ty read this text."

He handed me the phone, and it read: Tell Ty she full of shit. She didn't have to let me see her tonguing that no good mother fucker. What else she doing with him?

"What else I'm doing with him?"

"You read it for yourself; I didn't make it up."

"J Lamb, text him back."

"Text him from yo phone! Y'all ain't gone run my texts out, you just paid the bill."

I wanted to be furious, but you can't be angry with J Lamb. I got my phone and text back: *I wasn't doing anything. He plotted on you coming to see him doing that. I didn't kiss him.*

I sent the text and a few seconds later he text back: Yeah.

"J Lamb, he text back yeah."

"Well, yeah."

"Oh, hell, no, I am calling him."

"Call him, he ain't gonna pick up."

"Bet."

"What you want to bet?"

"If I am wrong, I will move in, but if you right you pay my phone bill again."

"How does any of that benefit me?"

"It don't. It ain't about you. You got other stuff going on. So, call him so I can know what I need to do."

"You need to shut up and stop hustling me."

"Hustling you? Girl, please."

"Yeah, please stop hustling me."

"We best friends, what are you talking about?"

I just looked at him as he said, "Hurry up call him, I want to hear what he has to say."

Giving my best friend no more thought, I dialed his number, and he did not answer. It went to voicemail.

"Which room is mine?"

"Boy, if you don't sit your ass down somewhere. I have a problem that you not helping me to fix."

We laughed as he said, "Let me help you then."

"The last time you said that; you showed me where they stayed."

"This time I am going over there and asking for him."

"I dare you."

"Ty, dare, drama, gossip and other names are my names so don't dare me to do what I want to do. I don't like her anyway."

"Why don't you like her?"

"I had her before Ahmad."

With a big, amused look, I asked "No, you didn't."

"Yes, I did. Remember I told you my girl is from Louisville, and her name is Trinity."

"Yeah, what you think the T in her middle name stands for, trifling?"

I laughed as I spoke, "What he doing with her?"

"If you ain't ever been with her, I can't explain it to you."

"You let her go?"

"You can't hold a real lollipop bitch down. She'll lick you up then go to the next sucker."

"J Lamb, I can't imagine you with her or any woman for that matter."

"You think I am gay like a lot of others, don't you?"

"Personally, since you are talking about it, it has never crossed my mind. I think you are bisexual, but for the most gay. So, are you?"

"Am I what?"

"Are you strictly dickly or what? I'm strictly dickly."

"I am what the mood calls for. If I feel slutty, I'm the slut, if I feel like a dominatrix, then I run the shit. Either way you can't lose with a lamb. For a lamb can represent innocence and purity, but if you don't do it right, she'll make you hate the day you didn't."

"Get out of here."

CHAPTER 12

I laughed as he walked towards his brother's place. Seconds later, J Lamb came back and said, "He said he'll be over in a few."

"You believe him?"

"Yeah, I believe him because you should have seen his face."

"What you tell him?"

"I told him in front of her; you need to talk to him about his real son because he won't answer the phone."

Smiling and grinning I had to ask, "What she say!"

"Nothing to me, and I think she knows better about trying to keep him from Josiah."

"Why you say that?"

"While you were gone, I was over there, and I was talking to you on speaker."

"You had me on speaker phone and didn't tell me?"

"If I told you, then it would not have been a sincere conversation."

"You dirty bastard you."

"Only call me those names in bed and I have no

intents of crawling in there with you ever, Tiger or not."

"Whatever."

"Nonetheless, I had you on speaker and he heard Josiah in the background saying momma you talking to daddy, and you said no daddy is gone. That touched him and I believe it was hearing you tell him that he was gone that made him realize that he messed up. Next thing I know he would pop up at the house wanting me to call you so he could hear y'alls voice. I think he was trying to see if another man was taking his place."

"You should have told me. He got to doing it so regularly, I forgot to tell you."

"I'm glad I didn't share any important information unless I called you."

"Girl, that wouldn't had stopped me, I still would have done it."

"Why?"

"You, my girl. He's, my guy. We all best friends and you always want what is best for your best friends. To me, you two are best for each other."

"I don't know about that."

"Tygeria, you don't ever know anything."

"Well, I don't."

I was laughing, but I was stunned, too. Almost all the time, I was talking to him I was on speaker. Thankfully, he and I didn't talk much, but how could I get mad, he use to do Ahmad like that for me. J Lamb said, "One day, she came in and heard you talking on the phone. She assumed he was talking to you and not me, so I put you on mute as they argued. He told her from that day forward that she will not stop him from talking to you about Josiah and how she has divided y'all enough and how no piece of ass in the world would ever come between him and his son again. And if she didn't like it, she can bounce like you did."

"Really!"

"Since then, he didn't call you because he didn't think you would talk to him, and he didn't think you would like Josiah talk to him."

"He did right. When I first left, I was consumed with anger that I would not have let our son talk to him but as time went by and I began to get over it, I would have, but he never called me."

"I think he wants you back. I mean the old you because this new you is something serious."

When he spoke that, a knock was heard at the door. I peeped out, and it was Ahmad. I was nervous and didn't know why. I opened the door, and he came in. He stood at the door and said, "Nothing is wrong with Josiah because I just left him."

"I want to talk about what you saw when you pulled

241

in the parking lot."

"All I saw was my wife kissing another man in my face."

"He was standing there talking, and the next thing I know, he was kissing me. I was stunned and couldn't move. Do you really think I would have done something like that?"

"I don't think you would have, but who knows? You come back here looking greater than you left, your weight is gone, and your confidence is at the roof, so I don't know what you are capable of doing."

"I haven't done anything since you. So why would I waste it on a man I don't know?"

"You went in his room chilling that night."

He is throwing that night up in my face, and I was shocked about it. I spoke, "We didn't do anything in that room but sat in those chairs separately, talking, and listening to music."

"That's not what he says."

"What you mean by that?"

"Never mind it's none of my business. All I ask is you keep your personal life away from Josiah. He doesn't need to be exposed to men like that."

"You come in here accusing me of something I

don't even know, when you are the one who hurt me and left us."

"You need to stop bringing up the past and go on. I am a changed man, and you are a changed woman, unquestionably."

"Say what you want. I have been loyal to you when you didn't need me to be."

"Didn't I say stop bringing up the past? Our son does not need us to argue in front of him, and all he could hear is about what happened back then."

"Then don't falsely accuse me of a man, I think of as only a friend."

With a strong sturdy face, Ahmad asked "And what kind of friends do you have?"

"Get the hell out my place, and the next time I leave Mississippi, I won't come back."

"I'll leave. You want me to call Devin and let him know you free or do you want me tell Blackie to come over, since he is closer? Then again, you have your men back-to-back anyway. I see the town's rubbing off on you."

Like that he left out.

J Lamb asked me blankly, "What he mean by that girl? You doing something and haven't told me?"

"Today on my lunch break, his friend hollered at

243

me, and I told him I will think about it."

"Friend? You talking about slow-looking Devin?"

"Yeah."

"My brother must be blind. Even I saw that you only did that for it to get back to him, and it did."

"My point exactly."

Another hour past and J Lamb said, "I have an idea."

"What's that?"

"Let's do our play."

I thought about it for a second then said, "You know we could get hurt for that?"

"Ty, no, we won't."

"Who is the victim?"

"That lying ass Blackie."

"I like the sound of that, but we can't do it today. Let's wait and do it on a Sunday."

"I ain't going to church on any Sunday, so you must be going? Anyway, just pick another day."

"Why not on a Sunday?"

"That's the Lord's Day."

"Every day is the Lord's Day, J Lamb."

"Yeah, but Sunday is the day we set aside to worship HIM, and I don't know if I can worship HIM on Sunday then on a Sunday night, do evil."

"You can't?"

"Yes, I can my bad, who am I fooling. I can."

The next few weeks were crazy. Josiah was with me on the weekends because I had trouble finding a sitter nearby. I didn't like it but I was doing what I have to do. At this point, Ahmad had started coming over to spend time with his son, and Josiah loved it. They would count and do everything that is taught at a Pre-K circle time. Ahmad said he wants to do all he could to make sure his son did not fall behind.

In his circle time, he happens to stress what is your daddy's name more and more. I believe he wants to make sure our son knows his name in case I am with another man. Either way, Josiah and Ahmad are happier. Even when he didn't have to, Ahmad would even stop by to bring Josiah stuff. Sometimes, when Josiah would sleep my husband and I would catch a movie or play checkers. Even during the week, when our son is at my brother's, he would come over, eat dinner, discuss Josiah and even flirt sexually with each other.

There were even times, Ahmad and I would talk about the Word of God or a dream. He would quote scriptures, and we would even discuss the meanings. Even when the topic was hard for us to talk about, we still maintained to have an open mind about married people having single friends. Either which way, I was smiling but still kept contact with Blackie for personal reasons; even though, I felt torn between the two.

Sometimes, I could tell that Ahmad didn't really like me communicating with Blackie so I kept if to a minimum. He and I were friends and that was about it. From time to time, he would ask to take me out, but I was always busy with Ahmad and Josiah.

On the other hand, I felt that Blackie was falling for me hard. It got to the point, where he was putting down on Ahmad more and more. It got so bad that I had to check Blackie. I had to let him know that Ahmad is still my husband and my son's father.

When Blackie stopped that, he started telling me stuff Ahmad had said about me or to his sister. I did not let that get to me but noticed that Blackie would mainly call when I was with Ahmad. I wasn't going to take the chance that Blackie was being bitter to ruin Josiah's happiness; therefore, I had to let what he said ride. Sometimes it was hard to ignore and brought tears to my eyes, but I had to be strong, I had to do it for my family.

I do admit after seeing the change in Blackie, it made me lean more to spend time with Ahmad. I didn't know what to think about this new relationship he and I were having, but Pastor Tatum told me to relax, for Ahmad is my husband. I am not sure if I should because my heart is at

246

stake, and I run a risk of being hurt far more than before.

Ahmad and I were seeking counseling from his dad and things were changing in my life. We were meeting up at church, sitting together, and doing all the things a family does. It was wonderful. Occasionally after a service, we would go to his dad's so Josiah would spend time on the farm which my husband loved as a child.

It made me happy to see my son content. Josiah was thriving and every night, Ahmad would read him a story like fathers do for their sons. I knew it was coming, and I wasn't amazed when Josiah kept inquiring for his father every day when he didn't see him.

All I had to do was tell Ahmad that Josiah wanted him, and he would come. He was spoiling him with his presence and giving me ideas that we could get back together and make this family work. Somehow, my husband would read my mind and give me comfort with a smile that says I still mean a lot to him.

He hadn't come out and said he wanted me back, but I was almost hoping it would come to that. When I cook, he eats at the table with us, like family. We teased each other and spent time with Josiah like parents do.

This husband of mine was making me fall deeper in love than ever, and it was working. He even talked to me on the job and the other men backed off. Ahmad would text me often, and it made me smile. There have been times when he would send me flowers and candy to my place and the workplace.

Ahmad was making his presence known and tensions were heating up. I wasn't sure how much longer I could hold out sexually. It has been too long over a year since I had a man, and I am leaning on my husband to be my first all over again. Every day I would tell J Lamb how Ahmad was acting. J Lamb stated, "What man would come around if the baby daddy still hanging around?"

I believe that is true, but he is still with her, so I don't get why hate on me. I know Bianca doesn't like it because she prank calls me. Finally, after service on Sunday, Ahmad was at in the room putting Josiah down for his evening nap. He came back in the living room with a smile. After being with this man for a long time, I know when he wants sex, and I just made up my mind to give it to him.

Ahmad stepped towards me and my phone rung. I held up my phone and said, "Look who calling me."

He looked at it and his smiled faded. "Don't answer it."

I didn't like the way he said it. To me he is already suspect because he comes over here in J Lamb's car and has on his jacket. Therefore, I did conclude that she doesn't know he was coming over to see his son. I didn't like it, but my son was happy and to see him happy meant, letting his father do what he had to do.

However, I ignored Ahmad and said to him, "I will put

it on speaker so don't say a word."

He began pacing the floor and rubbing his hands through in his hair. It made me uneasy but asked her anyway, "Why are you calling me?"

"Just to let you know that you are not winning Ahmad back just because he comes over. He is playing you but on another level."

"Why would I have to win back my own husband that I'm letting you use? And how is he playing me on another level?"

"You not letting me have anything, you fat bitch. He comes back and tells me everything. I know you cook and he eats there. He only does it so his son can see him being responsible. He doesn't want you, even if you are skinny now."

"You a woman and supposed to be grown woman at that and you want to be in grade school with the name calling?"

"I am telling you now ahead of time that he has to butter you up. Besides that, he has already put in for a divorce last week so we can get married."

My head jerked in his direction, as I lowered my eyes to say, "Marrying you?"

"Yup, he is marrying me and that is why the lawyer told him you will have thirty days to contest it. You should have received your papers by now; we gave him the right address."

Trying to sound hard I spoke, "The day I left is the day, we were divorced."

"He is doing it legally and then we will be rid of you. He hates that you try to flirt with him. He comes back here, and we make fun of you trying to be sexy and all. You still fat, and you still stank. To do things right, he is going to test my son. I also told him to test yours, too."

The mouth on my face flew open as I heard her say that. Ahmad had tears in his eyes, but that did not fade me. I am in dismay as I listened to her tell me things he could had told me. If she was lying, he would have had an altered reaction, but it was that of one being calm. Getting back to what she spoke, I questioned "Test mine for what? Josiah is his and if you look at him, you will see that for yourself, unlike yours."

"Don't worry, I have convinced him that during the time he was cheating you didn't cut up because you had been cheating long before him."

"You lying ass, conniving bitch."

"Name calling? Now who's grown?"

"Yes, I'm grown, and I don't have to break up a home to see if it can be done. Ahmad knows I don't have to lie to him. Ahmad knows I have never lied to him. I don't have to scheme and plot to make him choose pussy over

250

family."

"You come back in town still acting like you a diva, but you are still the fat girl that is in love and thinking he still wants you. Get it through your head, your divorce is on the way and all because you let him see that boy; silly notions are in his head about our son Brian."

"Well, is it?"

"Brian is more like Ahmad than your little piece of shit will ever be."

Ahmad began pacing the floor. He was angry when she said that about Josiah. I didn't know how to take this news. Seems like painful things have come from this woman, and I was always on the outside looking in. She is the one that told me how he thought of me. Now she is telling me that he is getting a divorce from me.

It was like the pain of him getting too close to me to hurt me was happening all over again. I let my guard down and he come in. Like a fool in love, I was the one playing house. First her brother places doubts and now her tongue has spun poison about me and Josiah. Ahmad looked at me and saw the tears as I dropped my head.

I am back in the same boat I just got out of; the only difference is it's a bigger boat. He sat beside me, and I got up. I was too angry, but I know she is not at home, but I will catch her when she comes in. Calmly I announced to her on the phone, "You are going to beg me for my help."

"Beg my ass. You can say what you want, DNA doesn't lie."

I hung up and asked, "So you been playing on my emotions all so you can divorce me and don't think Josiah is yours?"

"It's not like you think. I haven't been playing on your emotions. What I have been doing with you has been sincere. As for the blood testing, I'm just doing them both so can't no more be said."

"You divorcing me and really think that tall three-year-old is not your son, don't you?"

"I do know he is mine. I just want clarity on both ends."

"Endless things have come up since you've been involved with her. She wrecked our wedding day and now has planted lies in your head about your son and me. What is it going to take for you to see that Bitches over wives?"

"It ain't like that. She is not over you."

"How? She tells you want you want to hear, and you run with it. She has destroyed your life, and you are too blind and gullible to realize it. You defend her unwillingly to me, and you would rather destroy what we have than to leave her alone."

Out of nowhere, he stated "You act like you not a bitch. You act like you haven't hurt me."

"I became a bitch because a bitch rocked my world. But you want him tested although he looks more like you than you? Even though, I had never cheated on you, lied to you and only want you and you want to test our son?"

"I just said that so she will not fight me for a blood test."

"You beginning to say a lot when it comes to her and for her. When are you going to say things for me and my son? When will we be defended?"

"Ty, calm down and think rational."

Once again with my heart in my hand, I asked soberly "I have three questions for you. One, have you applied for a divorce?"

"Yes and no."

A tear out of dry eyes fell. I then asked, "Two, you want Josiah tested?"

"Yes."

"Three, do you love her more than me?"

"I don't know; I am confused. It's like I love you both."

"Since you don't know, I need to help you make up your mind. You believe Josiah may not be yours; I'll give you your test but until then don't come back over here for him again. When he asks for you, I will tell him he has

253

another family to go playhouse to."

"Don't do that, Ty. That's my boy."

"Your boy, the woman you lie for and pleases live in that other place."

"Ty, don't. I've already been out his life don't punish me anymore. We are doing so well."

With a fresh coat of tears in my eyes a crackle was in my tone as I said, "How about this? I am moving out this place, changing my number and divorcing you. So, you can be free from having to lie to me and for her. I'm out, now you get out."

Josiah must have heard me yelling as he came out his room crying, "No, daddy."

Ahmad looked up, and I shoved him on out the door. Josiah was bellowing the word, daddy, very loud as he cried. I know it hurt Ahmad because it was hurting me, too, but I didn't want him to say anything to my son ever again. He wanted Bianca and Brian then he can have them without the cost of my son's heart again.

All day it took a lot to get Josiah quiet. I felt like I was at the end of my rope. All the lies he told me about making it up to us was a bust. I called J Lamb and told him all about it and even he was at a loss for words. The only thing he said was, "The pussy good but it ain't that good" that kind of cheered me up.

The rest of that day went by nicely. During the next week, I took my son for the DNA test. It frustrated me to take him in for that, but this is something his father wanted. They told me the results will be back within a week, and I should receive my result by next Saturday. I wasn't pleased, but I was ready to get this over with. It became more evident that I must move on without my husband. I was doing all talk, but I have to really file for a divorce.

Every day I anticipated the blood test to be back, but it wasn't. I know Josiah is his, but I want to see it in writing so Ahmad can have the answer he seeks. On Friday, still no results. That afternoon, I went to see a lawyer, and he told me we could have had the marriage annulled because we never consummated the marriage. I had no idea that I could have done that, but silly notions of us being a family covered me and so did my ideology for revenge. I told the lawyer I will be back in, and we can go from there.

When that Saturday came, Josh came and picked up Josiah. I explained everything I been dealing with to him and Jessica. My brother was furious and doesn't want me to allow Josiah to see Ahmad again, but his wife persuaded him to think what if it was him. He said he understood what she was saying, but his little nephew has been through so much when it comes from his dad.

I had hoped Ahmad did not show up because my brother would have had some words with him. He didn't. Soon as Josh left with Josiah, I saw Blackie sitting on the small porch, and I called out for him. The more I stared at him, I thought about how he kissed me which had an impact on Ahmad's feelings. Dismissing the thoughts of his deceit; I have a role to carry out.

"I haven't seen you in a minute. You don't want to see me or something?"

"Naw, I was just waiting on you."

"My son is gone, and I need to be with a man tonight, any suggestions?"

Flashing those treacherous white teeth, he moved closer to say, "We can be friends with benefits, if that is what you are implying?"

"I have the urge to give myself to a man, and it can't be any man. He has to be one that will make me cry out for more."

"You know me, I know you, you married, and I have a friend why not try out this new cuddly buddy system and go from there."

"Dinner first at my place. Then maybe just maybe if you are a good boy, you may see these stripes."

"Text me when you ready so I won't be late."

"I will."

CHAPTER 13

Blackie laughed lightly. I thought, *they think I am a bitch. I am going to show them how a real bitch plays dirty ball.* Of course, the clothing for tonight has to be something sexual. J Lamb brought me over a costume, and when I saw the costume, I mean costume it was a costume for prostitutes. I had to ask, "Who going to wear this two-piece string set?"

"You are, but I don't want to see you in it, it could blind me. Please have on clothes when I see you again."

"You don't have to worry about that. Where you get this from?"

"It doesn't matter. All you need to do is turn him on."

Giving J Lamb the stare down, I said "You don't think I can do it alone?"

Placing his hand on my shoulder as if to give me a pep talk, he spoke "I'm not saying that; maybe I am BUT make sure he drinks all the wine."

"What you have in it?"

"Male enhancement."

"All that male enhancement won't hurt him, will it?"

"It's enough for him to take it all night long."

J Lamb and I laughed at that. I had to ask, "What man can take sex all night long?"

"With a little help, any man can."

"You make me think you have done this before without me?"

"Do you know or remember who you are talking too?"

"That is why I am asking" I said with amusement.

My best friend looked at me and said, "I hate you were hurt by them. I really do. It makes me really angry when bad things happen to good people."

"I know, but it happened, and I can't change it."

"You can't change it, but I can help it change."

"It was a lesson I had to learn."

"Right, but I know a real down for whatever bitch is in you somewhere."

We laughed as I said, "You just have your part ready."

"Ty, I have my part and then some."

"Then some? What you have planned?"

"I have something that will get results."

J Lamb left to get ready for his part to play. I went in the kitchen and began to put everything together. I had to make sure tonight was perfect. The feeling of Ahmad came all over me. It was like, he was going to mess everything up, and I don't need Ahmad coming over here. I must be sure there aren't any interruptions if this is to happen tonight.

I was going to have Blackie right where I want him, and I can't wait. When dark fell upon the day; I was already eager to put this into action, but I have to wait until the right time. I text J Lamb and told him that I have another hour before he is to come over. He texts back that he was excited for me. I checked on Josiah before getting off the phone. I made sure to cut the conversation short because Josh would get angry at Ahmad, and there would no telling what my brother would do.

My alarm went off and it was eight o'clock. I went in my room to get ready. Pinning my hair up, I rubbed cucumber melon lotion everywhere. Picking up the strawberry two-piece set, I eased on the bra first. It felt funny to be wearing a bra made like real strawberries that covered the nipples and top half of the breast. Once I slid on the strawberry patch panties, I wanted to laugh. The string in the back was like a thong, but the front was a strawberry patch with real strawberries.

Looking good enough to eat, I text for Blackie to come over. Being a bad ass, I opened the front door and stood in it, expecting to see Blackie. Making myself more delicious

I placed a jolly rancher in my mouth. To be more seductive, I rolled it side to side. My fear came true. When I opened my eyes, I saw Ahmad running towards me. He wasn't supposed to be there, and he wasn't supposed to come out the house.

Gathering my thoughts, I was about to close the door when he burst into it, sending me flying across the room. He grabbed the lock of my hair and wound it about his fist. He was breathing hard and panic struck me. He demanded an answer as he yelled, "What you doing dressed like that standing in the door?"

The only thing that came out was, "Get away from me, you smashing the strawberries."

"Damn those strawberries! I said what you doing dressed like that standing in the door?"

"Get your hands off me!"

He unraveled my hair one notch from his hands and asked, "Who is this for?"

"It's for the man that will be in here tonight."

"Who the hell is he?"

"Get out my place!"

"I am not going anywhere until I see the man that has signed his death certificate."

"Go back to Bianca. That is where your heart is at."

"You don't know anything."

"Oh yeah, I took Josiah for the DNA last week, and I talked to the lawyer about the divorce so from this day forward, I am no longer of your interest. You want your divorce; I am giving it to you, and you want Brian and Bianca, you can have them too."

Ahmad ignored me as he said with fury, "You are my wife, and I will kill you and him if I catch a man over here!"

He released all my hair. He got up and I shouted, "Go to Bianca remember you doing all this for her and the confusion you live in."

"I will not divorce you. You are my wife so whatever you have planned you better cancel it because you are mine!"

"Get the hell out of here talking about not divorcing me. Your wife and child live across the parking lot and after next week I won't live here either. So, get out and stay out."

Ahmad stormed away from me and slammed the door behind him. He sped away in his car and was gone. I didn't like the way he sped off, but he is his own man now and not my concern anymore. Trying to regain control of my emotions, I took deep breaths and thought about the task at hand.

When that came to my mind, how Ahmad acted was

261

no more. Seconds later, Blackie showed up. I opened the door, and he flashed those white teeth at me. I thought God how I love those white teeth, but quickly I got back on point.

"Don't just stand there and goggle at me, come in."

"I don't think dinner is on my mind right now, seeing you and smelling you like this."

He came in and I closed the door. He stood there waiting on me to walk by him and I did. He whistled and spoke, "Tiger, I like the way those stripes rip you up."

"You haven't seen anything yet, but let's have dinner first."

"I might want dessert, first."

"You might, but we have all night, what's the rush?"

I knew that if we go backwards, we will be off track, and all of this will be of no effect. I have to get back on course. After that stunt he pulled in front of Ahmad, I wouldn't have him, and it disappointed me. I was really into him and wanted him, but I wasn't into the game how he had played to me. The more I thought about what he did, the more I got into my role.

Blackie came behind me and began sniffing my neck, to break my thoughts. I removed myself from his grip and spoke, "I promised you dinner first, and that is what I plan to do."

"Sure, we have all night. I won't rush."

Walking seductively, he followed me to the kitchen. There on the table was a white tablecloth with flowers and candles as the center piece.

"This is nice."

"Thank you. I must feed you before I take care of you."

"Let us eat, drink, so we can explore the night."

We sat down and began to delight ourselves in the rice and sweet and sour chicken, egg rolls and wine. He and I talked. He drank for over an hour. His company has always been wonderful to me, but it also has been deadly to me. The more we talked and carried on I could tell he was getting to the point of wanting sex because he kept watching my huge breast.

I was fine with it because this was worn for him to feel this way. I got up, sat in his lap and placed my arms about his neck. This was fun and this is the first lap I sat in other than Ahmad's. It was weird but weird with a purpose. The minute all the wine was gone, I knew it was time. *Rubbing on him and allowing him to fondle me better be worth it*, I thought as I got off his lap to strip tease for him.

Blackie was tipsy and laughing. He was very turned on and in tuned with the dancing. He watched me as I danced to my bedroom. Quickly, I got my phone and place it by the bed. Just as I knew it, he came in behind me with his shirt off. Soon as he saw me standing there all perched up and ready. I said, "Let me finish undressing you."

Blackie allowed me to undress him, slowly. Too bad this isn't real for me. "Lay down on top of the covers, I want to tie you up," I spoke in a demanding tone.

"Kinky."

"That's right. I want to make sure when I take you, you can't buck me off you."

"If you are as good as I think I will stay there for you all night long."

"You think?"

"I know."

"You may not want this all night long."

"I've wanted you since I saw you at your apartment in Ackerman, and when Bianca got Ahmad, I knew I could have you in a matter of time."

"You are right. You will have me. In a few more minutes I am going to see what you going to do."

"Please every inch of you; that is what I am going to do."

"I hope so; I'm in need of a real man."

"You will have a real man not an irresponsible man like that so call husband of yours."

"Shush, too much talking and not enough sexing."

He obeyed me and got in the middle of the bed. Once he was laying there already for me, he said, "You going to turn off the lights?"

"No, I want you to see who is going to make you nut."

"Shit, I didn't know you were a down low lover?"

"I'm not; you will be my first."

"Hurry up and let me feel your mouth. You have no idea how long I have been waiting for you to do this to me."

"Hold on let me, get the satin cloths."

"Tiger, I like it already."

Blackie watched me tie him up. I had to make sure I tied him up tight because if I didn't, he would buck, and who knows what will happen if he comes loose early. Once I made sure he was tied, I put a tie in his mouth. I walked sexually to the end of the bed and said, "I am going to make sure you remember tonight for the rest of your life. I don't know what your precise role was when it came to my marriage, but this is for that day you kissed me in front of Ahmad. You plotted on the perfect timing for him to see you kissing me, but it looked like I was kissing you, too.

This night I hope you enjoy the line-up. Come on out."

Quickly, I put on my robe. Coming through the door was J Lamb and the guys from the club. I looked at Blackie and saw him shaking his head no. I wanted to be sorry for him, but no one was sorry for me when I was hurt. J Lamb pointed at Blackie and said with humor, "Have fun boys."

Getting close to Blackie's ear, J Lamb stated, "I don't know what they may have."

Blackie started bucking and bucking harder than ever. I knew if he could get up, he would, but that was not happening. I had never seen such filthy act. All I could think of was how he kissed me for a show. Out loud I spoke, "If you had never kissed me in front of Ahmad, we would still be cool now. You crossed the line and got in business that did not belong to you."

The first guy sat on him and began riding him, like a woman. I got some clothes and went in the bathroom to change. When I got back in the room, Blackie had an orgasm. The next guy began licking the nut. J Lamb said to Blackie, "The reason why you are hard like this is because of the Viagra in the wine. I knew these men needed you to do more than one nut. You greedy dog. Keep on drinking and drinking, following after pussy you don't know about."

I spoke to Blackie's tiresome face, "I would never put my mouth on you. Sleep with you for that matter. I might have had if you and your sister weren't underhanded."

266

About an hour passed, and Blackie was worn out before the final piece came. When, the last guy came in the house he had at gun point, Bianca. I was surprised. She was tied up and naked. I looked at J Lamb and asked, "What she doing here?"

"This is my own treat."

"What you mean?"

"She is going to fuck her own brother."

My mouth flew open, and I stammered out the word, "Why?"

"Because she fucked my brother when I loved her; therefore, tonight she is going to know what it really means to fuck in the family."

"J Lamb, I don't know about that. Our objective was to get Blackie back for kissing me on purpose. She is a great touch I might add, but it's not worth it."

"Ty, you are not a real bitch; I am. You have heart when it comes to people that have wronged you, I don't. People like her don't care about what they do to people; they only want to do what they want and damn the rest. Today I say the rest is damned."

"J Lamb, I was a hurt by a woman like that, too, but I am doing better."

"Let me do this. You are declared innocent after tonight she will no longer mess with you and Ahmad.

Josiah's name won't come out her mouth."

The guy pushed her closer to Blackie and through the tie in her mouth; I heard her say, "Please don't."

I remember I told her she will ask me for my help. On the other hand, I was compelled be her saying please. From her actions, I didn't want to make her suffer. "J Lamb, it's not right. Let her go."

"You right, she should taste him first."

"I didn't say that."

"I know you didn't. I just assumed it came out your mouth wrong."

"She may try and press charges for holding her at gun point."

"She won't because like I said bitches only tell shit about other bitches and not themselves."

A few seconds flew by as J Lamb asked, "So you want me to let her go after she slept with your husband, my brother?"

"I do because this isn't right about her sleeping with her brother. It's morally wrong."

"It is if you are in the church, but I don't go to church, do I?"

"Come on. You my best friend and I always back

you but don't do it."

"Did she not do it on your wedding day? Did she not do it, when she called you taunting you? Did she not do it, when she made me fall for her then she started screwing my brother? Did she not do it, when she called Josiah that little piece of shit? Which reminds me, the DNA test came back, and the baby is not Ahmad's, it's mine."

He threw me off guard as I caught the last end of his paragraph. "What you a daddy?"

"I know right."

"Brian, isn't Ahmad's?"

"Nope."

So many emotions rushed through me as I finally know that her son is not my husbands at all. In haste, I asked "Does he know?"

"Yeah, he knows, and he was mad because he has lost you and Josiah over this bitch right here" he said as he pointed to Bianca.

"My brother lost a year of could have been happiness because she wanted it all."

He got in her face and yelled, "But you can't have it all BITCH!"

"Let her go. She will no longer be involved in my life. It's over with. I saw Blackie hurt and that's it."

"I just wish I could give you back the time she made you and Josiah lose."

"Just let her go."

"She can't pull on him one time?"

"No, J Lamb, I'm sure she has gotten the message."

"I don't know. Women like her will play like they understand, but as soon as she gets out of this jam, she will be doing her old tricks again. I say let her sleep with him. Who agrees?"

Those men were agreeing with him. For some reason, J Lamb is really adamant about making an example out of her. Out loud I asked, "She must have really hurt you?"

"She did; the worst part is I loved her."

"You have a child with her."

"And? She used that child as a toy to keep my brother in line. The more I think about it the more I want her to sleep with her brother, like she slept with mine."

"Ahmad did what he wanted to do. He's at fault, just like her."

"He is, but he is my brother. He didn't know she was the same girl like you didn't until tonight. I left him sitting in the yard, drinking, and listening to your wedding songs. Girl, go get your husband. He has been without you for too long, and you know like I know he is a weak-minded bitch."

I saw a tear roll down her eyes. I walked to her taunting her by saying, "I told you that you will ask for my help, and I'm not giving it to you. Fuck your brother, because you fucked his. And when you finish fucking your brother, I hope they all fuck you. By the way, I was a wife before I was a bitch. Now it's bitches over wives and I have the power."

With a surprise in his voice and a yes in his nod, J Lamb spoke "You have heart after all."

J Lamb pointed for the guy to pick her. Bianca was resistant, but when he showed her the gun she complied and sat on Blackie. She didn't move, but J Lamb said, "Work that dick like you would Ahmad's. We all know you aren't a stiff fuck."

Gradually, she began to move on him like a lover. Blackie just laid there dazed as he stared at J Lamb. I left out because it didn't matter anymore. I was finally free of them all. Moments later, Blackie came out of my room. He didn't say anything to me, and I didn't expect him too. Next the men came out, but no J Lamb and Bianca. I got up and went to the mailbox. Why did I not think about the mail earlier was beyond me.

I went back inside and sat at the kitchen table. I saw the diagnostic address. No idea as to why I was nervous, but I was. I opened the letter and saw that Josiah was ninety-nine point five percent Ahmad's. I literally began crying. There was never a doubt, and here is the proof. It was as if a weight had been lifted off me. If I wanted child support and freedom, I had it.

It's funny how you can be close to someone, and they still pull the wool over your eyes. I never knew J Lamb was in love with Bianca because he used to call her T. It also never occurred to me until now how on my wedding day, they were arguing like they knew each other. They did; I just didn't know they did.

And after all this time of getting over Ahmad, I loved him all the more; even though, he was living with a woman and allowing her to direct him at her will. If you don't know what love is, one can get confused and mistake one thing for another. To me it was no excuse, being a ruthless bitch was more important than being a sweet wife because being a bitch carried weight.

Not just weight but power. I needed to have the weight she had because it made my husband do crazy things. Making up my mind to go see Ahmad and confess some things; I ran back into my room for my cell. Soon as I picked it up, I noticed Bianca and J Lamb having sex. I slammed the door and went to my car.

Opening the phone, there was a missed call from Pastor Tatum. The time was thirty minutes ago. I called him back and he said, "Can you come to the Choctaw Medical Center, right now?"

Instantly I felt panic striking me. Hurriedly I asked,

"Is something wrong?"

"Ahmad had a wreck and other than me you are the rightfully next of kin; they need to see you if the need be."

My heart sunk. I became dizzy. With my phone in my hand, I stumbled out my car shouting, "J Lamb! J Lamb!" as I ran back into the house crying and being hysterical.

He came out the room, and I don't know if he was naked or not but all I could say was, "Ahmad wreck."

J Lamb rushed over to me and yelled out, "What!"

"What? Who told you?"

"Your dad. Choctaw hospital."

J Lamb placed his arms above my elbows and questioned, "Ahmad in Choctaw General?"

All I could do was shake my head, yes. J Lamb looked as if he saw a ghost. He walked around a few minutes in a circle as to get his thoughts together. I wanted to move, but my feet would not allow me to. I could think about was how everything that I had done to get him to see that he loved me didn't matter anymore.

CHAPTER 14

J Lamb ran out the house and jumped in his car with me right behind him. I didn't care about locking up my apartment. All I knew was I had to get to Ahmad. Thrusting on the blinkers, I drove as fast as my vehicle would allow, and I still could not catch J Lamb. He made it a few minutes before me. When I got there, seeing a vacant parking spot near the front, I slammed the vehicle in park, jumped out leaving the door open and engine running.

Pastor Tatum was the first one I saw, and J Lamb was acting up wanting to go see Ahmad, but no one was allowed. Security came and told him to settle down before they take him to jail or make him leave. Pastor Tatum had a hard time getting J Lamb to be quiet as he walked him outside.

Seconds later Pastor Tatum came over and gave me a hug. I asked, "Where did J Lamb go?"

"I told him to put a shirt on and cool off. His brother and others here do not need him acting up."

"You know J Lamb can be something serious when it comes to Ahmad; that's his only sibling."

"I know."

We were quiet a little longer as Pastor Tatum said, "Josh is on his way over."

I was glad to hear that because my brother has always been my biggest supporter, if I ever needed one. All I could do was tremble before asking, "What did the police say happened?"

"They said a dog ran out in front of him. He swerved off the road into the football stadium here and hit the concrete concession stand by the entrance. The impact caused the air bags to pop out as it crushed him inside the car. The people that saw it called for help as quickly as they could."

"Has the doctor been out yet?"

"No, the doctor hasn't come out yet, but you do know that whatever is happening, he is in God's hand?"

I gave him a faint grin as I dropped my head. Pastor Tatum gave me another encouraging squeeze as I asked, "What happened to make him leave your house?"

"He came home and was mad because he said you were about to make love to another man. He wants to kill you, the guy and him. He kept saying that he has taken all he could and tonight it was going to stop. I had never seen him so angry before, but I talked him out of it."

"Was all this before J Lamb came to my house?"

"Yes, he was taking a shower and getting ready to come to your house. Ahmad came in ranting and raving to show us the letter that stated that Bianca's little boy was not his. Jamal came out his room and opened his letter. He showed us that the boy was his."

"J Lamb really did take a DNA test?"

"Yeah, said Bianca told him that the little boy could be his, so he took the test to shut her up. To tell you the truth, she wasn't quite sure who the daddy could be. Being that Ahmad was an easy target; she put it on him. When this happened, I sat my sons down and told them not to let this come between them. Jamal was thoughtless about the situation. I guess neither one of us thought about how much a toll this would be on Ahmad. Think about it, he has lost over a year of Josiah's life and happiness with his longtime love."

I began to feel water in my eyes as I said, "I love him, and I don't want him to die."

Pastor Tatum placed his arms around me and allowed me to cry on his shoulder. My brother came in. I rushed to him as he gave me a familiar hug. Whispering confidence, Josh said "He's going to be ok, Ty. You have to believe that. The Lord is in control of everything."

I didn't answer him. Josh let me go and walked with me to a seat near Pastor. Before sitting down, the men spoke and remained quiet. Josh touched my hand to encourage me. Nothing came to my mind but how I love him. My brother being the big brother he is, knew what I was thinking as he said, "Sis, I know you love him. He is your husband, and you suppose to. What kind of wife would you be if you didn't truly love the man you married?"

I didn't say anything as Josh asked, "Does anyone want coffee?"

Pastor shook his head, no, and I didn't answer. Josh got up and said, "Let me go get me some coffee. It may be a long night."

Josh went to get some coffee. Pastor said, "I wish I saw the signs before this evening."

"You saw what you needed to see."

"Tygeria, I thought once he discovered the truth about the little boy, you and he could make it work, but I had no clue just how hurt he was. Ahmad always kept his feelings inward, unless he wants you to see it."

"We can't change it."

"I know better than anyone, but he has been fighting to uncover how to do right, since your wedding day. There have been times he said he wish he could rewrite that day and never laid eyes on her, but he can't. Tygeria, my son has and still loves you."

"How?"

"I can't explain it like you want to hear, but he has not stopped loving you that is why Bianca tried so hard to keep you both a part. She knew he would never love her like he loves you so she taunted you. She had to make you leave him alone because he was not going to leave you alone."

J Lamb came in the waiting room. This time he had on a jacket as he sat down on the other side of his dad. For ten minutes we did not say a word. To break the ice, J Lamb said as sincere as I had ever heard him, "Dad, we need to pray as a family for my brother. He has everything waiting on him, and he doesn't need to be away from his son anymore. I will give my life for his."

"Son, we can pray the Will of the Lord but to swap one life for another is not the Will of God. Neither you nor I can say who needs to live or die. Since your brother is in here, he is the one the Lord wants in there. If HE didn't want Ahmad in there, trust me he wouldn't be."

"But dad."

"You have good intentions son but keep them as intentions because only God is in charge no matter what it looks like or how we want things to be. He holds life and death in his hands, and no man on earth can do no more than Christ allows. Do you understand?"

J Lamb must have taken in what his father said because his tone changed as he asked, "Well can we pray for God's Will then?"

We met Josh in the hall as we were going to the sanctuary to pray. He put the coffee down and came in with us. That made me so happy that my brother put his feelings aside to be in this with us for there is strength in numbers. We all held hands as Pastor Tatum began to pray for the will of Christ. Honestly, everything went unheard.

I was so focused on Ahmad that I did not hear the prayer itself. From deep inside, I was making a vow. If he lives, I would change my ways. Nothing is as important as making sure he lives. Even if he has some impairments, that would be fine because he was still alive. Shortly after we came out of prayer, Josh stated, "I know I haven't cared for your husband since the day of your wedding, but I do care if he lives. I am your family, and so is he."

"Josh, that is so good to hear. Thank you."

We went back to the waiting area. The doctor came out and asked for the next of kin and I stood up as everyone positioned themselves to hear what the doctor had to say. Pastor Tatum held one of my hands as my brother held the other. Preparing myself to hear, the worse the doctor said, "He is banged up badly with swelling and may have a concussion. To be on the safe side, I'm keeping him overnight for further observation because internal bleeding could show up, and we want him here if that be the case. If everything checks out alright, he'll be able to go home tomorrow."

J Lamb asked before I could, "When can we see him?"

"He will be going in a room within an hour or so. Once he gets settled in, you all are welcome to go see him."

"Thank you, doctor."

He nodded and walked off. We all did a group hug. Pastor Tatum spoke, "God is an on- time God, and I am assured that he heard our prayers."

I was happy, and so was everyone. Josh told me he was going home to let Jessica know. I told him not to tell Josiah because he would be crying for his daddy. He agreed as he left us. J Lamb gave me a hug and said, "I want to you to be in there when I talk to him in the morning."

J Lamb and I broke off the embrace and walked a few paces. I asked, "Ok, now tell me about you having sex with Bianca?"

"Oh that?"

"Yes, I want a new set of sheets for sleeping with her in my bed."

"Where you going to get them from, I don't have a job?"

"You better take them off my bed and buy me some more when you get your last check."

"You late, I been got that."

Pastor Tatum came over and said, "We can go in and see him now, but his face is covered up because the lights hurt his eyes."

J Lamb looked at me. I was nervous as I placed my feet upon the floor slowly. J Lamb halted me as I was about to enter the door to say, "Don't take your ass in there boo-hooing, his ass going to be alright."

"I'm not. Just don't you ass start boo-hooing."

His father looked back at us, and we stopped our conversation. When the door to the room opened up, Ahmad was asleep, with his head pointing to the left of the bed and his feet towards the TV. We didn't wake him because he needs his rest, but tomorrow when he wakes up he has some explaining to do. J Lamb and I took a seat on the short couch. Pastor Tatum leaned between us and said, "I'm about to go home to get some sleep. Call me if you need me."

"Ok, we will."

Pastor smiled at me and walked out the room. J Lamb said, "Why you lie to daddy for?"

"I didn't lie. We will call him if we need him."

"No, you said we, I didn't say me."

We laughed silently as we fell asleep waiting for Ahmad to come around. Often during the night, I sat and watched the back of his head. I thought about my life with him, and how I loved me some kind of him. He was my world and, in a sense, it was fucked up and broken.

The next morning, Pastor came in. J Lamb and I got up and walked to the right side of him, which faced the door so Pastor could sit on the couch. Ahmad moved a little and his head turned towards the couch as it became uncovered.

J Lamb and I waited because Ahmad turned around to face us before we left out. J Lamb and I both jumped back and shouted, "Damn."

Pastor Tatum gave us that look to shut us up, but it was too late. J Lamb spoke, "Brother, you look like you stole honey with bees still in the nest, but I am glad you will look better than what you look now."

Ahmad still did not say a word. It was uncomfortable to be in here with him. Tapping J Lamb's foot with my foot, I was letting him know that I was leaving. Backing back some, I began to walk off. Ahmad opened his mouth to speak. I could not understand his dry tone for J Lamb said, "Tygeria, wait, my dummy said to stay."

"Jamal," Pastor Tatum said to his son.

Jamal said, "He did say stay. I'm standing right here by him."

I stopped and Pastor said, "I will leave out so the three of you can talk."

Pastor left out, and we all were alone. J Lamb asked, "Can I go first?"

Ahmad did not say a word. I said, "Knock yourself out."

J Lamb sat on the bed towards Ahmad's feet and said, "Brother I was scared when I found out about your wreck.

No piece of ass even if it's a good piece of ass, I might add should come between us. You were wrong for leaving my girl, Ty and sleeping with the only woman I had loved. Anyway, that's water under the bridge. Tell your wife the truth and make things right."

Ahmad words were clearer, "Don't make mistakes like me."

"Nigga, I ain't you. You stupid. I even been telling Tiger Ho that for years, but her ass was all caught up in your ass, she thought I was just running my mouth."

I cut in to say, "Like you doing now?"

"I guess so. Can I stay and listen?"

"No, J Lamb, this is personal" I said.

"How personal is it when you are going to tell me what he said, and he is going to tell me what you said. Cut the middleman out and let me sit in so you won't have to repeat it and leave stuff out."

Grinning, I humped my shoulders. Ahmad sat up in bed as J Lamb sat on the couch. I sat on the bed where J Lamb had sat. My husband asked in a better tone, "Josiah know?"

"No, I don't want him to know anything like that. He would panic-stricken to see you in here like that."

We were quiet and I said, "If you are not up to talking, we can do it later. I don't want to stress you."

J Lamb cut me off as he yelled out, "Oh hell, no. Stress my ass. Y'all need to do this now while I ain't got nothing to do."

"If you keep butting in, you will get second-hand conversation."

"Let me shut up, because Ahmad half talk and you leave shit out. I can't stand that, telling me some of the conversation today and remembering what you left out next week."

He saw that we weren't speaking as he said, "Go on, Ty, you said if he doesn't feel like talking y'all can talk later."

I chuckled as Ahmad said, "I want you to know I am so sorry for all the pain I caused you. I see now for myself that you have loved me with everything you have, and I took it for granted. It might not look like it, but I never really stop praying for guidance from the Lord. I ask you today as a man ask the woman, he loves to please find it in your heart to forgive."

Glancing at J Lamb, he spoke, "What? I didn't ask you to forgive me, he did. Answer the question. I want to know."

"I forgive you; I just won't forget."

"Won't forget?"

"No, I won't forget."

"I know it is too soon" Ahmad added.

"It's not that but I have been through a ride with you and forgetting is up in the air."

Ahmad stared at me as he touched my hand. I pulled away because to have him touch me was awkward. I wasn't sure if I was ready to feel him touch me. He showed me his wedding hand and spoke, "I only took my ring off when I saw you because I didn't want you to know that I was still claiming to be a husband. From the way you reacted, I feel that you may not want to be my wife anymore."

I didn't say a word and then he asked sympathetically, "Do you want to be my wife, Tygeria?"

"I never stopped being your wife; I just didn't have a husband to be a wife to."

"I am ready to be with you and only you. I am more ready than ever."

As if I were praying, I placed my hands to my mouth. I stood up and stated, "A year ago I dreamed of this very moment and now it's here. When Bianca came to our wedding, all you had to do was stay with me so we could work things out as husband and wife. You didn't see fit to understand that Josiah, and I needed you just as much as she did with her unborn son."

"I can't get back what is gone forever, but I can start over by renewing our vows. Daddy said he will do it; all we have to do say, yes, and put this behind us like a memory."

"Are you patronizing me?"

He spoke louder as he replied, "I would never do such a thing to you. I have always loved you. I would even tell her that I love my wife."

"You love me! Love is a four-letter word like piss, hate, fuck and shit."

J Lamb said, "Ooh."

I continued by saying, "It almost took losing you to realize that I already lost you. When you left me minutes after marrying me, you showed me that you didn't give a damn about me or what I thought. After all this time, I've been holding on to a myth of what I thought loving someone should be like. And for me to be as ruthless and frank as I am, I have you and Bianca to thank. So, you take your piss, hate, fuck and shit on to love the next bitch because I don't think I am the one."

His mouth dropped open as I rolled my eyes at him and left out his room. I did not want to give him a chance to weasel out of owning up to his faults. Truth be told, I didn't want to hear anything he had to say. J Lamb came out the room like a F5 tornado. He spun me around and spoke with surprise, "If I wasn't in there to hear it with my own two ears, I wouldn't believe it."

"Believe it, I said it to him."

J Lamb dropped his hands from me as he asked, "Didn't he say the right words? Didn't you want to hear him say he wants you back and how he sees his mistake?"

"At some point, that is what I always thought I wanted to hear."

"Well new bitch, what are your plans now?"

"My new purpose in life is to fuck up as many homes as these bitches allow me to."

As if he were disappointed, he stated "You don't mean that."

"Why not? A bitch ruined my home and destroyed what I believed. Why not teach other hoes lessons that no one took time to teach me?"

"You accomplished what you wanted, and I know you can't change and be the old you but go back to church."

"J Lamb, church? I have done too much to go back to church and too much has been done to me for church. Besides, the people will look at me funny, and you know it."

"You have had just as much church training as I have so you know that people are going to be people. You could do all the good in the world, and they will still say something wrong with you. So, Ty, don't give me that lame excuse. There's nothing to it, but to do it, right?"

"I guess."

"There's nothing to guess about. I know that innocent church girl is still in there."

"If she is, she is deep in there."

"It's not that deep or too low that God can't reach down and pull it up. Plus don't you miss hearing what God has to say through your leader, when you are too busy to listen to HIM yourself? I know you still pray and fast to some extent."

With excitement, I spoke "I do and somewhere along the way I have lost sight of the big picture, but it's the way the pastor gives the uncut Word of God. It helps convicts you or makes you realize what you are doing is wrong."

"Well, you must position yourself to receive what God has for you. If I am not mistaken, all this you went through was a testimony for someone else. Sometimes we are placed in situations just to be able to tell someone how you overcome it. It does not make it right, but that is just how it is. You may have to tell some other woman how you took your husband back after all he had done to you and yet you did that. Sure, you may not have done it exactly right, but you did that and who knows."

I turned away from him because as crazy as he is, he was making sense. I did do all of this just for him to wake up and see that I am the only woman for him. Yet it took a car wreck for him to see that I love him more than I was willing to admit. I thought about how hysterical I was when I heard about his wreck.

Facing J Lamb I spoke, "I don't know. It's like I want to do right but doing wrong covers me because I have done wrong for so long. Who wants to play with God by half going to church?"

"You haven't done wrong that long but even if you have, God is a forgiving God and coming back to him is the best thing you can do. You won't be playing with him by not having it all together. That is the common mistake. People think they have to have the perfect clothes or stop doing whatever sin they do before they can go to church, but they are wrong. It's when you don't go that you are playing with God. It's when you make stupid excuses that you play with God. If you come as you are, HE will supply all the other stuff you need."

"I'm going to start going back to church that is no question. I have to; my life has fallen apart, and I don't know how to pick up the pieces. Not to mention there has been so much I have been through and to think, I almost killed myself. Jamal. I was at the brink of destruction. I prayed in the church for the Lord to intervene. If I hadn't, I would have pulled the trigger. The Lord allowed Josiah woke up out the car to see me just when I was about to blow the top off my head off."

"Tell me God isn't on time because HIS time is never ours, just like now. Turn from your ways and move on. We can't change what has happened, but we can change what happens from here. No matter how we do things people will find a way to make you feel bad but that is when you have to die out to how you feel about things anyway."

I was quiet for a few minutes until he practically screamed, "Answer me this, do you still love that man God gave you?"

With tears upon me, I spoke with clarity and loudly, "I will always love him. Ahmad has been the love of my life for all my life."

"Well give it another try and bury that new bitch."

Pointing back at Ahmad's room, J Lamb demanded, "Go back in there and get your husband. He needs you more than ever. If you walk away from him now, then you don't know what kind of life you could have had. Think of your son and how it would mean the world for him to grow up in a two-parent household. Remember the love you have and do your best to make it work."

"But I am tired of always putting the needs of others ahead of my own. I am tired of being last."

"You are not, and you know when you had that little guy that your life became a standstill sort of speak. But with Christ, we all have been bought with a price that neither one of us could repay. I love you, and I only want what is best for you and my brother."

"What is the best?"

"Only God can answer the fullness of that, but haven't you both suffered enough from the hands of the enemy? Look at me and tell me you don't want to be with that fool of a brother of mine and I will let it ride? Tell me you don't love him anymore and you will let it all go because of how you feel."

I couldn't look at him and lie because no matter how my new attitude is, lying has never been a part of my character. Tears began to swell in my eyes as I leaned on J Lamb's shoulder and cried. In my ear, I heard him say, "Get back right with God and go in there to your husband. Some people don't get a second chance because they die in their mess, or a second chance never comes. But you, you have them both. Don't waste any more time than you both already have."

Pulling me back he said, "What you say, Ty?"

"I say, I'm going to go get my husband."

Shaking my head, I wiped the tears from my face and walked back towards the room. When I opened the door, Ahmad saw me and sat up in bed. I strolled towards him and kissed him . Pulling back, I said, "You look horrible."

"As long as you love me and will have me, I don't care how horrible I look."

"Mr. Tatum, I guess you are in luck. Your wife is back and loves you more than ever."

EPILOGUE

Tygeria and Ahmad, learned to forgive and move on. Later on they remarried and rededicated their lives to God.

J Lamb became a minister and took his son from Bianca for she didn't want to raise the child anymore.

Blackie did not go back to his wife. He moved out of town because he didn't want what happened to him to get out.

www.ingramcontent.com/pod-product-compliance
Lightning Source LLC
Chambersburg PA
CBHW021505240626
47154CB00002B/510